THE FAERIE PAWN

DARK WORLD: THE FAERIE GAMES 2

MICHELLE MADOW

DREAMSCAPE PUBLISHING

SELENA

THE MOMENT after snatching the golden Emperor of the Villa wreath and becoming the winner of the first Faerie Games competition, I regretted it.

Because as the Empress of the Villa, I had to send three of the ten other players to the arena at the end of the week.

One of them would die in the fight. The other two would live.

The two who lived would have a serious grudge against me.

One of the privileges of being Empress of the Villa for the week was that I got to stay in the most luxurious suite on the second floor of the mansion. Other players could spend time with me there, and thanks to a spell from Vesta, we wouldn't have to worry about being walked in on or our conversations being overheard.

Julian and Cassia were with me in the suite. Cassia was relaxing next to me on the huge king-sized canopy bed, leaning back into the comfy pillows. Her green wings glowed brightly behind her. Julian sat across from us, on the magnificent sofa that looked like something straight out of the palace of Versailles.

They were helping me figure out who I should send to the arena.

"Octavia told me during the welcome banquet that she was coming for me," I said. "She has to be the one to go."

I frowned, my stomach swirling. Because I was talking about *murder*. I was going to send two other players into the arena with Octavia in the hope that they'd kill her.

It's self-preservation, I justified to myself. *If I don't do this, Octavia will come after me. She'll make sure I'm killed.*

No matter how many times I told myself that, it still didn't make it any less twisted and wrong.

But if I didn't select three players for the arena, I'd be breaking the rules of the Games. The gods didn't take kindly to players breaking the rules. I doubted Juno would be so lenient with me a second time.

However, I still had options. Everyone always had

options. I'd read somewhere that just because you disliked your options, it didn't mean you didn't have them.

I could sacrifice myself. I could stand up there with the entire Otherworld watching and refuse to select three players to send to the arena. I could make my point, and be killed for it.

But I didn't want to die. I was only sixteen years old. There was so much more I wanted to do with my life.

Plus, Prince Devyn had advised me to trust my instincts. And every bone in my body told me to do whatever was necessary to live.

"Selena," Cassia said, looking at me strangely. "What do you think about that idea?"

I must have spaced out. "What idea?" I asked.

"Mercury's champion—Emmet—has it out for us after we fought against him to get that horse," she said. "He's a strong fighter. He has what it takes to beat Octavia. Put another strong player in there with them, and you should be golden."

"Are you saying that I should talk to Emmet—and the other player I choose to go to the arena—and ask them to work together to take out Octavia?"

"Yes," Julian chimed in. "Emmet and whoever else you choose can be pawns to get Octavia out this week."

"And if I let them know they're pawns, they might be

less likely to come after me later," I said, remembering the lesson that one of my trainers, Bryan, had given me before I'd entered the villa. "Especially if I make a deal with them that benefits them in the next few weeks of the Games."

"Exactly." Julian nodded, his ice blue eyes as hard as steel. It was slightly unnerving. But as the champion chosen by Mars, battle strategy came naturally to him.

I couldn't help but find his confidence ridiculously attractive. But I pushed my feelings as far down as possible. Julian didn't care about me, and he never had. From the moment we'd met at the end of Torrence's driveway, he'd used me just as he was advising me to use the others.

I couldn't let myself forget that.

"The third champion should be Felix," Julian continued. "It'll be just what he needs to let him know his place in the Games."

"His 'place?'" I asked, recalling how Julian had acted all territorial when Felix had talked to me and Cassia on day one. Well, when Felix had *flirted* with me and Cassia. "What exactly is his 'place?'"

"He thinks he can use his magic to get into the hearts of all the females in the Games and manipulate them into doing whatever he wants," he said, each word clipped and angry. "Sending him to the arena—and talking to him privately to make sure he knows he's a pawn—will show him that you won't fall for his tricks."

As we spoke, the glowing, golden orbs buzzed around us, recording every moment of the conversation. The viewers must have been eating it up like candy.

"What kind of history is there between you two?" I asked.

"There's no history," he said.

"So why'd you act so weirdly toward him when he was talking to me and Cassia in the library?"

"Because he was using his magic on you," he said quickly. "His magic makes him dangerous."

"His magic didn't work on me." I sat straighter.

"Not *yet*." Julian narrowed his eyes, like he was challenging me to continue being immune to Felix's magic. "But it will eventually. Venus's champions excel in using their magic to convince the opposite sex—or anyone else attracted to them—not to send them to the arena. It gets them far every time. Some have even won because in the final fight, they've used their magic to make the other person love them so much that that person takes their own life instead of battling it out. Felix's magic is more dangerous than you realize."

"But he's not a physical threat," I said. "He didn't even try to fight anyone for a horse in the Emperor of the Villa competition. He just let Octavia take him with her."

"Then why would he be on board with the plan to take Octavia out?" Cassia asked. "Obviously there's something going on between them."

Was it just me, or did she sound hurt when she said that?

Hopefully she wasn't falling for Felix already.

"Felix might have Octavia wrapped around his finger," Julian said, although Octavia didn't seem like the type to get wrapped around *anyone's* finger. "But from what we know about Venus's champions, he doesn't return those feelings. He's using her. I'm sure he'll be on board with the plan, since it means saving his own skin."

"What about Cillian?" Cassia said. "He has some of the strongest magic in the Games. If anyone has what it takes to take out Octavia, it's him."

"Cillian isn't someone I want on my bad side." I shuddered just from thinking about it—and because of the warnings my trainers had given me regarding Pluto's champions. They were notorious for being unhinged. "Plus, he doesn't seem open to deals with anyone. If I send him to the arena, he'll survive and come after me later."

"He will," Julian agreed, his eyes fierce. "You can't send him to the arena."

My stomach fluttered at the intensity in his voice. It

was almost like he couldn't bear the thought of me being in danger.

Which was silly. Because everyone playing in the Games was in danger.

It was just a question of who'd die sooner, and who'd die later.

Before I could respond with another suggestion, someone knocked on the door.

I walked over to look through the peephole. It was Pierce—Vulcan's chosen champion. He was a big guy, with muscles so huge that the veins popped out of them.

Yet, Julian had beaten Pierce in their sword fight for a horse in the Emperor of the Villa competition. The image of Pierce on the ground with the bottom halves of his arms lying lifelessly next to him still hadn't left my mind. I didn't think it ever would.

I opened the door, although I didn't let Pierce in. "Hi," I said, hoping I sounded casual. "What's up?"

He glanced at the ceiling and scratched his head. "What do you mean?"

Right. The faeries had left Earth for the Otherworld in the fifth century. Their language had progressed alongside ours, because their realm existed parallel to ours. But they didn't know modern-day slang.

"Sorry." I stifled a chuckle. "I mean, what's going on?"

He glanced at Julian and Cassia. "I was hoping to speak with you alone."

"Of course." I opened the door to let him in. "Julian and Cassia were just leaving."

With that, Julian and Cassia stood up to leave my suite.

Julian gave me a final look over his shoulder—like a warning—before leaving me alone with Pierce.

2

SELENA

PIERCE STROLLED in like he owned the place and plopped down on the sofa where Julian had previously been sitting.

I straightened my empress wreath and perched on the end of my bed, waiting for him to tell me why he'd come.

"I know that you, Julian, and Cassia worked together to defeat Cerberus." He stared at me head on, like he was challenging me to deny it.

"Why do you think that?" I asked instead, not ready to confirm or deny.

"Don't act stupid," he said, and I sat back, stunned at how strongly he was going on the offensive. Especially since I was the one deciding who to send to the arena this week. "Octavia and Felix were the last two to arrive at the Tomb before you, Cassia, and Julian. They saw all the players who'd gotten there beforehand, unconscious from Cerberus's blood. Which means it had to have been you, Julian, and Cassia. We all know. So you can stop pretending otherwise."

The golden orbs hummed closer to our faces now, clearly loving the tension.

"Fine." I squared my shoulders, refusing to let Pierce intimidate me. "You're right. Julian, Cassia, and I teamed up to get past Cerberus."

"So the three of you are working together?"

"We teamed up to get past Cerberus," I repeated, even though I knew what he meant. He wanted to know if the three of us were in an alliance.

As if I'd give away any alliances I'd made that easily.

"The three of you had to have made a deal—at least for this week." He leaned forward and rested his elbows on his thighs. "You wouldn't send either of them to the arena after working together like that. And you definitely wouldn't send Cassia to the arena, since the two of you fought Emmet together and shared a horse."

I kept my expression neutral. Because he was right.

But not about all of it.

He—and apparently all the other players—didn't know that Bridget had told us how to get past Cerberus.

Which meant they didn't know that the *four* of us had a deal, and not the three of us.

"I'm weighing my options," I said casually, avoiding answering his question. Unlike full-blooded fae, half-bloods *could* lie. But I'd always prided myself on being an honest person. My biggest lie had been when I'd pretended to be Torrence to sneak out of Avalon, and look how *that* had turned out. So I didn't want to lie in the Games until it was absolutely necessary.

It *would* be necessary, at some point. My trainers had warned me that no champion had ever won the Games without lying. But I still wanted to avoid it as much as possible.

"Good." He nodded.

"Did you have anything else you wanted to discuss?" I asked, trying to politely end the conversation.

I wanted him out of my suite.

"You heard what Julian told me when I let him have that horse, right?" he asked, his eyes gleaming.

I pressed my lips together. Pierce had hardly "let" Julian have that horse. But I *had* heard their conversation right afterward.

"Julian promised that if he won Emperor of the Villa this week, he wouldn't send you to the arena."

"Yep." Pierce lit up a fireball in his hand, passing it back and forth from one hand to another. The fire reflected in his eyes, and his message was clear. Anyone who messed with him would get burned. "Since you needed Julian's help to get Empress of the Week, I think it would make sense for that deal to still stand."

It took all of my effort not to scowl.

Instead, I called on my lightning, feeling it crackle and pop under my skin. But when I tried to form a bolt between my hands, nothing happened. It was like my magic had a mind of its own, refusing to show itself unless I was under extreme duress.

I lowered my hands, not wanting Pierce to see my weakness. "Right after submitting to Julian, you came after me and Cassia," I reminded him.

"I had to try," he said. "I'd look weak if I didn't try."

"Maybe."

The more I talked to him, the more I realized that even if I asked him to work with Emmet to take out Octavia, I wouldn't trust him to follow through on his word. Octavia, Emmet, and Pierce were ruthless and out for themselves. The third person I chose had to be a team player.

Pierce wasn't that person.

His fire burned higher, from both hands now. "You might not be willing to promise that you won't send me to the arena, but I can promise you this," he said, his face a mask of deadly calm. "If you send me to the arena, I won't be the one who loses. And I'll be coming for you. You're a wild card, Selena. Everyone's already threatened by you. The last thing you need is another player gunning for you."

"And if I don't send you to the arena?" I raised an eyebrow, challenging him to give me a good offer.

He snuffed out the flames, smoke drifting up above his head. "If you don't send me to the arena, I'll return the favor if I win Emperor of the Villa."

I nodded, although at this point, I might as well push it even farther. "And will you do your best to make sure your allies don't send me to the arena if they win?" I asked.

"I don't have an alliance," he said, which I knew was a lie. I'd seen him with Emmet and Octavia enough to know they were close. It was also why I couldn't be sure what the three of them would do if they were in the arena together. "But if anyone I have sway over gets Emperor of the Week, I'll do my best to convince them not to send you to the arena," he continued. "Although at the end of the day, I don't control them. They're going to do whatever they want."

"But you'll try," I said.

"You have my word."

I knew to only take his word with a grain of salt. But

this was a good deal. It wouldn't do me any good to let him think I doubted him.

"Thanks." I gave him what I hoped was a friendly smile. "I'm glad we had this talk."

"Me, too." He studied me, as if wondering how far he could push this. "Now that we have that covered, who are you thinking about sending to the arena?"

"I haven't decided yet," I said, since it wasn't a lie. I still had no idea who the third person was going to be.

All I knew was that I had to take my shot at Octavia before she could take a shot at me.

3

TORRENCE

Two days.

That was how long it had been since I'd seen Selena.

Those two days felt like a lifetime. My worry for my best friend and my guilt for pushing her to go to Earth consumed me. If I hadn't given her that stupid transformation potion, she never would have been kidnapped to the Otherworld. She'd still be home on Avalon, where she belonged.

Queen Annika and Prince Jacen were right when they said I thought I was above the rules. I'd always thought rules were meant to be broken. Breaking them was exciting—thrilling, even.

I wasn't big on admitting my mistakes. But now I stood in front of the Earth Angel's door, ready to do just that.

I took a deep breath, trying to calm the butterflies going crazy in my stomach. Then I raised my hand and knocked.

The doors swung open. The Earth Angel and the three mages sat around the fireplace, old books open on the coffee table between them.

She and the mages were the only ones other than myself, Jacen, and Bella who knew the true story—that Selena, Jacen, and Bella had not left on a short vacation to finally show Selena the world beyond Avalon. Of course the Earth Angel needed to seek comfort somewhere.

Just as I did.

The mages wore their typical medieval style dresses, while the Earth Angel was casual as always in jeans and a t-shirt. In moments like these, I had to remind myself that despite *looking* nineteen, the Earth Angel was actually way older.

Her sharp golden eyes met mine, her powerful aura descending upon me. Worry for her daughter was etched all over her face. "Torrence," she said, her voice hollow when she said my name.

My heart sank into my stomach. She hated me.

"Earth Angel." I lowered my head slightly in respect, although really, I was just glad to have a reason to look away from her. "I was hoping to speak with you in private."

"No." The word was sharp and abrupt. "Anything you have to say to me can be said in front of Dahlia, Iris, and Violet."

I twisted my hands together and shuffled in place. Apologies weren't exactly a strength of mine. And now I had an audience of four instead of one.

Iris raised her hand, and green magic burst out of it, shutting the doors behind me with a bang that made me jump in place. "Say what you came here to say," she said. "The sooner you're out with it, the sooner we can return to our research."

"All right." I stood straighter and met the Earth Angel's eyes. "I keep thinking about what you told me the other night, and you were right. I've always thought I'm above the rules. But after what happened to Selena, I realize that most of the time, the rules might be there for a reason."

"Most of the time?" The Earth Angel raised an eyebrow.

"Yeah." My cheeks heated. "I mean, sometimes rules are made by bad people. I suppose they have their reasons for those rules, although that doesn't mean they should be followed. But you and Prince Jacen want to keep everyone on Avalon safe. I shouldn't have questioned that. I'm sorry I did."

Much to my surprise, the Earth Angel gave me a hint of a smile. "You're right," she said. "When bad people put rules in place, it's best to do everything possible to rebel against them. We should never be complacent. I wouldn't be here right now if I'd ever been."

I knew she was referring to how she'd escaped her life as a human blood slave in the vampire kingdom of the Vale to become the powerful force she was today. Her story was a legend on Avalon.

"I also have to take responsibility for my own faults," she continued. "I've always believed that rules should be explained and understood by those expected to follow them. Unfortunately, because of my blood oath with Camelia, I was unable to do that for Selena. And it's *possible* that when I was your age, if I were in your situation, I might have done the same thing you did."

I stood there for a second, stunned. "So... does that mean you don't hate me?" I asked.

"I never hated you," she said sadly. "I just wish all of this never happened. I hate the situation. Not you."

"I hate the situation, too," I said, glad the apology was done with so we could move on to more important things. "Have you heard anything from Prince Jacen and Aunt Bella?"

"Not yet." She glanced at the books spread out on the table. "But we've been checking in on them through the tracking rings we gave them before they left."

"So they're safe." If they weren't, I assumed the Earth Angel and the mages would be panicking.

"They're still at the crossroads."

"But they left almost twenty-four hours ago."

Dahlia rolled her eyes. "We know that," she said. "And if there was a problem, they would have texted us. Right now, our most important job is to research the fae, so we're prepared for anything they might throw at us."

"There isn't much written about them, so it's a challenge," Iris chimed in. "But we're finding bits and pieces."

I frowned. That didn't sound promising.

"I want to go to the crossroads to check on them," I said. "The five of us in this room are the only ones who know what's going on, and you guys can't leave Avalon since your magic is bound to the island. I'm the only one who can leave. So I'm going."

The four of them looked at each other in question.

Waiting was killing me. Because the truth was, I was probably going to go to the crossroads whether the Earth Angel said yes or not. Which would be super hypocritical after everything I'd said about realizing that not all rules were bad. And I really *had* meant it. But I also hated sitting around when I could be doing some-thing to help.

"Good idea," the Earth Angel said, stopping me right before I started to argue about why I should be allowed to go. "But on one condition."

"Anything," I said, since at this point, I was just grateful to be given permission to help Selena.

"We don't know what'll be waiting for you at the crossroads," she said. "So I'll be sending the Queen of Swords with you to protect you."

4

TORRENCE

MY EYES WIDENED. The Queen of Swords was as much of a legend as the Earth Angel.

She was also the most powerful warrior on the island, and she was scary as hell.

"Well?" The Earth Angel tilted her head. "Do you agree to the condition?"

"I do," I said. The Queen of Swords might be a fierce warrior, but I was the strongest witch born in decades. Sure, the Queen of Swords and I had only seen each other in passing, but I'd never been shy. I had this. "But does the Queen of Swords know what actually happened to Selena?"

"Not yet," she said. "I'm about to fill her in. Iris, you'll come with me, since you're the only one of us not bound to Camelia's blood oath and can speak about what's happening. Once we're done, we'll bring the Queen of Swords back to my quarters, and the two of you can head out. So... wait here. This shouldn't take long."

The Earth Angel gave Iris a knowing look. Then the two of them flashed out, leaving me alone with Dahlia and Violet.

I walked over to where the mages were sitting and plopped down in one of the chairs. "So," I said, looking at the piles of books on the table. "What've you all learned about the fae?"

Despite all the books, the mages knew practically nothing about the fae.

No wonder the Earth Angel was so quick to jump on my offer to check in on Prince Jacen and Aunt Bella.

The Earth Angel and Iris popped back in about forty-five minutes later. The Queen of Swords stood between them.

Like mostly everyone else on Avalon, the Queen of Swords appeared to be in her mid-twenties, thanks to the anti-aging effects of the food and water on the island. She wore her black Avalon workout gear, and her long red hair was pulled back into a ponytail. Since she was a Nephilim, her eyes were the same sharp gold as the Earth Angel's. Her gleaming sword—*the* Holy Sword, Excalibur—was sheathed at her side.

I'd seen her fight with that sword before. It was incredible—like she and the sword were one and the same.

"Hi." She looked me up and down, as if appraising what she'd be working with. "You must be Torrence."

"Yep." I squared my shoulders. "And you're the Queen of Swords."

"I am." Her eyes sparkled with amusement. "Although the title can be a bit of a mouthful. Just call me Raven."

My mouth nearly dropped open. The last thing I'd expected to happen today was to suddenly be on a first-name basis with the Queen of Swords. But here I was. So I might as well go with it.

"Hi, Raven." I did my best not to sound mind-blown about addressing the Queen of Swords so casually, although I totally failed.

"Annika filled me in on what's happening with Selena," she continued, jumping straight to the point. "We both trust that Jacen and Bella have the situation under control. But it can't hurt to check up on them. Although we'll have to do so undetected, since we don't want to interrupt anything important that Jacen and Bella might be doing. Which means we'll put on cloaking rings and drink invisibility potion before leaving. Sound good?"

"Sounds good," I said, relieved to finally be doing *something* to help Selena.

"Great." She smiled, looking surprisingly friendly for someone so lethal. "Let's get ready, and then we'll head out."

5

SELENA

I COULD BARELY EAT the next morning at breakfast. The anxiety swirling in my stomach took away any appetite I might have had. Luckily, Octavia and her friends did most of the talking, so I was able to sit back, study everyone, and weigh my options.

After the meal, Cassia and Julian followed me up to my suite. We didn't even have time to start discussing my conversation with Pierce before someone knocked on the door.

Felix.

Curious about what he wanted, I let him in.

Every muscle in Julian's body tightened the moment Felix entered. He looked like he wanted to punch Felix in his unnaturally handsome face.

Felix ignored Julian and hopped onto the bed, situating himself between me and Cassia. His pink wings shared space with both of ours, sending a spark of unease through my body.

Cassia pulled her hair over her shoulders and scooted closer to Felix.

I inched away until I was as close to the edge of the bed as I could get without falling off.

"What do you want?" Julian asked Felix, not bothering with pleasantries.

"Just some time with the two most beautiful ladies in the villa." Felix crossed one leg lazily over the other, not looking like he was going anywhere anytime soon. "It isn't fair that you're getting them all to yourself."

I rolled my eyes and crossed my legs *away* from him.

Felix turned to me and moved closer. "So," he said. "Any chance I can get some time alone with you to chat?"

I shuddered at the request, even though I *should* have asked Julian and Cassia to step out so I could hear whatever Felix had to say. It was normal for the Empress of the Villa to have one-on-ones with every player before selecting who was going to the arena.

But I could tell that Felix expected me to easily give in to his request. And I hated the way he stared down at me, like I was a puppet that would bend to his will.

I wanted him to know I was stronger than that.

But before I could say no, Julian cracked his knuckles and stood up. "Go for it," he said. "I was about to head to the courtyard to work out, anyway." He marched out of the suite and slammed the door shut so hard that a crack formed down the middle of it.

One of the golden orbs buzzed straight through the door to follow him. Once it was gone, the crack quickly repaired itself, thanks to Vesta's magic.

"You should go with him," Felix said to Cassia. "I'll come down and find you in a bit."

Cassia stared up at Felix, entranced. I had a feeling she was about to do whatever he asked. But then she turned to me, her green eyes questioning. Like she was asking if I wanted to be left alone with Felix or not.

Relief coursed through me the moment she resisted his magic.

"Go ahead," I told her, since whatever hold Felix had on others didn't seem to affect me. "I'll join you guys once we're done up here."

Cassia nodded and headed toward the door, although she did give Felix one final longing look before leaving.

That was *not* good. But I'd chat with her about Felix later. Right now, I had to focus on the conversation at hand.

"So." Felix smiled at me mischievously. "What's gotten into Julian?"

"I have no idea." I stared at the sofa where Julian had been sitting, as confused by his outburst as Felix. For someone who'd claimed there was no bad blood between them, he sure wasn't acting like it.

"No matter." Felix moved closer to me. "Now that it's just us, I'm looking forward to hearing who you're intending to send to the arena this week."

I balked at the forwardness of his question—like he expected me to answer without hesitation.

What an arrogant jerk.

"I'm still thinking about my options." I studied my nails, making it clear that I intended to tell him nothing.

"Come on." His eyes were playful now, his voice more musical than ever. "You can trust me not to tell anyone."

"Not even Octavia?" I challenged. "Because the two of you looked awfully close when she pulled you up onto that horse with her."

"Don't be jealous of Octavia," he teased, brushing his finger against my forearm. "She has nothing on you."

I yanked my arm away, glaring at him for having the nerve to touch me like that. "I'm not jealous of Octavia."

He looked startled by my resistance, but only for a second. "Good," he said, his eyes soft and understanding.

"Because there's nothing going on between me and Octavia. I simply took what was offered when she pulled me up to share her horse. Can you blame me?"

He might have been an arrogant jerk. But he *did* have a point.

"I guess not," I said. "But even once I decide who I'm sending to the arena, I'm not telling anyone until the Selection Ceremony. I don't want to worry anyone unnecessarily."

He studied me for a few more seconds, like he was waiting for me to change my mind.

"Was there anything else you wanted to talk about?" I asked.

His face hardened, and he sat back so there was a normal amount of space between us.

Finally, I could breathe again.

"My magic doesn't work on you at all." He stared at me like I was some sort of anomaly. "Does it?"

"It doesn't," I admitted, since there was no point in hiding it anymore. Unlike Felix, I had no intention of flirting my way to the end of the Games. "It never has."

"So you fancy women then?"

"No." My thoughts immediately went to the kiss I'd shared with Julian back on Earth—when I'd thought he was just a regular human. "Definitely not."

"Hm." Confusion passed over Felix's eyes. "That's

strange. My magic works on anyone who fancies men. Unless…" He paused, a light looking like it had gone on in his mind.

"Unless what?"

"Unless you've met your soulmate," he said simply.

I laughed, since that was the last thing I'd expected him to say. "Half-bloods don't have soulmates," I said. "You know that."

"Half-bloods *rarely* have soulmates," he corrected me, as sly as ever. "But it's happened before. And it's the only explanation for your immunity to my magic. So that has to be it. Tell me. Who is it?"

Wow. He was a bigger gossip than Torrence. And she loved to gossip, so that was really saying something.

"I don't have a soulmate." I laughed and waved away his idea, despite the pit of worry growing in my stomach. "There are tons of other possible reasons for why I'm immune to your magic."

"Like what?" He crossed his arms in challenge.

"Like my biological mother being a witch instead of a human," I said quickly, continuing before he had a chance to argue back. "Or the fact that I grew up on Avalon instead of in the Otherworld. Or it could be a side effect of being chosen by Jupiter. Who knows? But I don't have a soulmate. I'd know it if I did."

Each explanation sounded logical as I said it.

But the clawing feeling in my gut made me wonder if Felix could be right. Which was ridiculous. Because the only person I'd ever felt that way about was Julian.

And Julian had betrayed me in the worst way imaginable when he'd kidnapped me to the Otherworld.

He couldn't be my soulmate. He wouldn't have done that to me if he was.

Felix simply sat back and waited, like he knew I was about to crack.

Luckily, a knock on the door brought me back into focus.

"I should get that." I jumped off the bed and opened the door, not even bothering to look out the peephole first.

Bridget stood in front of me, holding an overflowing plate of cheese, bread, and fruit. Her gray eyes were big and innocent, but it had to be an act. Bridget was Minerva's chosen champion—the goddess of wisdom and strategy. One of her gifts was prophecy.

She must have known I needed this interruption.

"I noticed you didn't eat much at breakfast," she said. "I thought you might be hungry."

"Thanks." I smiled, and my stomach growled. I wasn't sure what I was more grateful for—the food or the interruption. "Perfect timing. Felix was just leaving."

Felix stood up and circled close to me, as smooth and

graceful as a cat. "Good chat," he said, placing his hand on my shoulder with a friendliness we definitely didn't share. "But yes, I was just heading out. I don't want to leave Cassia waiting for me for too long."

He waggled his eyebrows and breezed out the door, leaving both me and Bridget scowling in his wake.

6

SELENA

BRIDGET PLACED the fruit on the coffee table and sat down on the couch. I moved over to the chair next to her and put a piece of cheese on top of a small slice of bread to make an open-faced sandwich.

"So." Bridget popped a date into her mouth, chewed, and swallowed. "What are you thinking of doing this week?"

I quickly told her the idea about sending Emmet and another player to the arena as pawns to take down Octavia.

"Smart." Her eyes glinted with approval. "As long as he knows he's a pawn, Emmet will most likely be happy to have everyone watching him so he can show off his strength."

"That's what I was hoping," I said, relieved at Bridget's confirmation that my gut feeling was correct.

"Guys can be so empty headed like that." She rolled her eyes, and I smiled, since that was definitely something we agreed upon. "The third player you send in should be Pierce."

I froze at how confidently she said it, and the comfortable feeling between the two of us disappeared in an instant. "I'm not so sure about that," I said, lowering the cheese sandwich and summarizing the conversation I'd had with Pierce last night. I purposefully left out the part where he'd offered me safety, since there was no need to share *everything* with her. "He's dangerous and I don't think I should send him to the arena yet," I finished. "Not when there are other options."

"It should be Pierce." She leaned forward, her intense gaze locked on mine. "Trust me on this. Put Pierce in that arena, and you'll get what you want."

"You know that for sure?"

"Well, the future's never set in stone," she said, which I already knew, since she wasn't the first prophet I'd met. "But it's a highly likely outcome."

"That's good to know." I continued eating my food, thinking about it. Because she might be right that if I put

Pierce in there with Emmet and Octavia, the guys would work together to take Octavia down.

But after my conversation with Pierce, I didn't want to send him to the arena. There had to be a better option.

"Putting Pierce aside," I said. "Who else do you think would be willing to work with Emmet?"

Her gold wings fluttered with panic. "With everyone else, the future's up in the air," she said. "It has to be Pierce."

I gnawed on a fig, since the only person I truly trusted in the Games was Cassia. Despite my three-week deal with Bridget, I couldn't fully trust her.

I believed that sending Pierce to the arena would get me what I wanted *this* week. But what about the weeks further out? What if sending Pierce to the arena would result in my own death when he came after me, and would give Bridget a better chance of winning the Games?

At the end of the day, everyone was looking out for themselves. I couldn't let myself forget that.

I sighed, my wings heavy with the weight of the decision I needed to make. "Are you sure there's no one else I should be considering?" I asked.

"One of my gifts from Minerva is prophecy," she said, as if I needed reminding. "Trust me. I'm sure."

I didn't believe her.

"What about Cillian?" I asked, testing her. "He's one of the most powerful players in the Games."

"Not Cillian." She shuddered, her eyes darkening. "Definitely don't send Cillian to the arena. Everyone will pay for it if you do."

Goosebumps rose on my arms, my chest hollow with fear. There was something deeply ominous about her tone.

"It's a lot to think about," I finally said.

"I know." She quieted and chewed on her lower lip, and I wondered if there was something she wasn't telling me. But then she reached for a grape and popped it into her mouth, returning to her normal calm and confident self. "You should go down there and mingle," she said. "It looks bad if the Empress of the Villa stays in her suite for the entire week. Distancing yourself from the other players will only hurt you in the long run."

"I know," I said, since my trainers had told me the same thing. "And I will. But first, I want to finish eating. There's no way I can go down there on an empty stomach."

"Isn't that the truth," Bridget said, and just like that, the tension between us disappeared.

As we ate, we chatted about normal things, like the

differences between the Otherworld and Avalon. But my mind was somewhere else.

Because Bridget wanted me to send Pierce to the arena. Julian wanted me to send Felix to the arena. Cassia had told me she'd stand by whatever decision I thought was best.

Everyone wanted what was best for *their* game. Which wasn't surprising.

It served as a reminder that I needed to figure this out on my own. And I only had two days to do it.

After I finished breakfast, I'd go downstairs and feel out some of the other players to get an idea about where their heads were. I'd get some one-on-one time with everyone but Octavia before the Selection Ceremony.

Once I did that, I'd have a better idea about who I trusted, and what move I was going to make.

7

TORRENCE

THE QUEEN OF SWORDS and I drank from the same batch of invisibility potion, so I could still see her and she could still see me. She looked hazy and had a bit of a glow to her—like a ghost—but she was still there. I knew from looking down at my body that I looked the same.

Since Nephilim couldn't teleport, I took her hands and blinked us to the crossroads.

We arrived seconds later. We were standing at the bottom of a hill, grassy land stretching out around us as far as the eye could see.

The crossroads were nowhere in sight.

The Queen of Swords took out her cell phone and searched for our location. She held the phone up and took a few steps around the area, apparently having trouble getting service. "We're about a mile away," she finally said, looking back at me in shock. "Good job."

"You didn't think I could do it?"

"The Earth Angel and the mages believed you could," she said. "But you're young, and teleporting to a place you've never visited before is a skill that not even many adult witches can master."

"I'm the strongest witch at the academy," I said, proud of myself for impressing the Queen of Swords.

"I see that." She smiled again. "I guess I'm kept so busy training the Nephilim that I don't have time to keep tabs on everyone else on the island."

"Except for the wolves," I pointed out, since the Queen of Swords was mated to one of the wolves. Her mate was another legend—Noah of the Vale. Their souls had combined when they'd mated, so both of them were a mix of Nephilim *and* shifter. They were the first of their kind, although a few on Avalon had followed suit afterward.

"Of course." She winked. "You know I can't get enough of the wolves."

I stilled, shocked. Was the Queen of Swords *bantering* with me?

She totally was.

But as entertaining as it was to be talking with the

Queen of Swords like we were actually friends, we had more important fish to fry.

"Which way is the crossroads?" I asked.

"That way." She pointed in a direction as grassy and empty as everywhere else around the area.

"Then let's go."

As we got closer to the dot on the Queen of Swords' map, a glowing green dome of magic appeared over the horizon where the crossroads were supposed to be. It was a massive eyesore, and it seemed out of place in a location that was supposed to be somewhat under the radar.

"Is that normal?" I asked, since no one had warned us about any kind of boundary spell around the area.

"I'm not sure." She scrunched her forehead. "I've never been to the crossroads before."

"What?" I stopped in my tracks. "They sent you to come with me, and you've never even *been there* before?"

"Chill." She laughed. "When there's something to worry about, I'll take my time to assess the situation and decide what to do."

"And that's not something to worry about?" I tilted my head toward the glowing green dome that *definitely* hadn't been mentioned in the part of the book the mages had shown me about how to call for the fae at the crossroads.

"That's just a boundary spell—it's not going to attack us," the Queen of Swords said. "We'll get closer, but not *so* close that whoever's inside might see our footsteps in the grass. And remember—the crossroads are fae territory. The fae are known for being tricky. We have to be skeptical of anything we see in there."

"Will do," I said, continuing toward the dome.

The Queen of Swords was quickly by my side, her red ponytail bouncing as she walked.

As we got closer to the dome, we saw the hazy shapes of two people inside. I looked at the Queen of Swords in question. She nodded to continue our approach, quickening her steps.

The dome was relatively translucent, so it wasn't long before we could make out the people inside.

Prince Jacen and Aunt Bella.

Prince Jacen was pacing around, his features knotted in deep concentration. Aunt Bella sat on a rock near the lake, looking bored as she scraped the outside of a large stick with her dagger.

It looked like they were *stuck* inside the dome—like the dome was a spherical prison. Why else would they be hanging around inside of it? It wasn't like either of them to sit around doing nothing when Selena's life was at stake.

"It's just the two of them," I whispered to the Queen of Swords. "We should talk to them. They might have information about Selena that we can bring back to Avalon."

Prince Jacen's head perked up, and he stopped pacing. "Hello?" he asked, looking in my general direction. "Is someone there?"

The Queen of Swords glared at me. I pressed my lips together and took a step back. But she gripped my arm, and the message was clear. Don't move.

Now that Prince Jacen and Aunt Bella were looking our way, they'd see our footmarks in the grass.

Aunt Bella's eyes locked on the place where we were standing. She dropped the stick, held her dagger at the ready, and walked toward the edge of the dome. "Show yourselves," she commanded.

"They might not be able to hear us," Prince Jacen said.

"Maybe not." She raised her dagger and hit it against the inside of the dome. It didn't ripple, like a dome created by a witch would have done. "But they have to understand this." She slammed her dagger against the dome again, and again, and again.

That was my Aunt Bella for you. She never held back.

Prince Jacen walked over and grabbed her wrist, stopping her from slamming her dagger into the dome again. "That's not helping anything."

"Maybe not." She shrugged. "But it's not hurting anything, either. Which is unfortunate, because we need to get out of here."

"Let's try the peaceful method first." Prince Jacen stared at her until she lowered the blade.

Once the blade was down, he placed his hand against the dome. "We've been trapped in here for almost a day," he spoke in our general direction. "The fae did this to us and left us here. If you can hear us, please, come forward. We need you to get a message to Avalon."

I glanced over at the Queen of Swords. She stared straight at Prince Jacen and Aunt Bella, not budging. Her face was hard as stone and completely unreadable.

Did she think there were fae hiding out in the dome? That the fae were spying on the dome? That Prince Jacen and Aunt Bella were fae in disguise? That last one couldn't be it. I knew Aunt Bella anywhere—no fae in disguise could imitate her so perfectly.

Whatever the Queen of Swords was thinking, I didn't care. Prince Jacen and Aunt Bella needed help, and they had information about Selena. We couldn't just stand there and do nothing.

So I reached for the antidote pill inside my pocket, popping it into my mouth before the Queen of Swords had a chance to stop me.

8

TORRENCE

"TORRENCE!" Aunt Bella said as I shimmered into view. "It's about time someone came to check in."

I rushed forward and placed my hand on the outside of the dome. It felt as solid as a glass wall and emanated warmth. It didn't bend slightly like a boundary spell cast by a witch would have done.

"I was worried after not hearing from you for so long," I said. "The Earth Angel gave me permission to come."

Before I could ask about Selena, red hair flashed in the corner of my eye. The Queen of Swords. She'd taken her antidote pill as well, and was no longer invisible.

"Raven," Aunt Bella greeted her. "Glad to see that Annika didn't send my niece to the crossroads without a chaperone."

"Not like it mattered." The Queen of Swords glanced at me, and surprisingly, she didn't look pissed that I'd revealed myself without her permission. "Torrence has a mind of her own."

"She takes after her aunt that way," Aunt Bella said proudly. "Anyway, this thing blocks our magic and cell service, otherwise we would have contacted Avalon by now. Any chance the two of you know how to get us out?"

"Unfortunately, no." The Queen of Swords pressed her palm against the dome, then pulled it back. "Do you guys know if anyone is listening to this conversation?"

"Not to our knowledge," Prince Jacen said. "The faerie I called for came here, trapped us, and left."

"That makes no sense," I said, and all eyes turned to me. "I was just looking through books with the mages to learn more about the fae. The mages don't know much, but the one thing they *do* know is that the crossroads is neutral territory. When anyone meets with the fae at the crossroads, neither party can do anything to the other that wasn't agreed upon in an official deal made there."

"Did the mages tell you that you're only supposed to call on the fae on the full moon?" he asked.

"They did. But the faerie came when you called, so obviously the spell worked when the moon wasn't full."

"The reason you're not supposed to call on the fae

when the moon isn't full isn't because the fae won't come," he said. "It's because the crossroads is no longer neutral territory when the moon isn't full. The fae can do whatever they want to people who call for them on all other nights. Like imprisoning them in a dome."

The Queen of Swords reached for Excalibur's handle. "I've broken out of a dome before," she said. "No reason why I can't do it again." She glanced at me, her golden eyes set in determination. "Stand back," she said. Then she turned back to Prince Jacen and Aunt Bella. "You guys, too."

I automatically did as she said. "What are you—"

She cut off my question by raising Excalibur above her head and smashing the flaming blade into the dome with an insane amount of supernatural force.

Bolts of electricity shot across the entire dome. It was so bright that I needed to shield my eyes.

When the electricity fizzled out, the dome was the same as before.

"So much for that," the Queen of Swords said.

I stepped forward again, focused on Prince Jacen and Aunt Bella. "Does the message you need us to get to Avalon have to do with Selena?" I asked.

"The fae have her," Prince Jacen said. "Just like we suspected."

I cursed and bit down on my lower lip. "There has to be a way to get to her," I said. "Right?"

"Not that we know of," Aunt Bella said.

"The faerie that came to us—Nessa—wasn't open to any sort of deal," Prince Jacen said. "But before she left, she told us some important information."

From the dark look in his eyes, we weren't going to like what he was going to say next.

"What is it?" the Queen of Swords asked.

"Time doesn't always flow the same way in the Otherworld as it does on Earth," he said. "According to Nessa, time is moving faster there. For every day that passes on Earth, an entire week passes in the Otherworld."

His words crashed over me like an icy wave. Because Selena was taken sometime Saturday night.

Today was Monday.

I cursed again, horror filling my bones as I quickly did the math. "Almost two weeks have passed for her there," I said.

"Yes," Prince Jacen confirmed.

"We need to find another way to get to the Other-world," I said. "As quickly as we can."

"Before coming here, we spoke with our allies and looked through as many texts on the fae as we could," Aunt Bella said. "We have no records of any ways to enter the Otherworld. The crossroads are the only way to contact the fae."

Defeated silence fell upon us.

"You said you asked your allies and searched through books," the Queen of Swords finally said. "But did anyone go to my mother? The *prophetess* of Avalon?"

"Your mother couldn't locate Avalon back when she was under Azazel's control," Aunt Bella said. "What makes you think she'd be able to locate the Otherworld now?"

"She might not be able to locate it," the Queen of Swords said. "But maybe she can lead us to someone who can."

9

TORRENCE

THE QUEEN OF SWORDS and I told Prince Jacen and Aunt Bella that we'd send more witches to try taking down the dome, and then I teleported us back to Avalon.

The Earth Angel waited anxiously in her quarters. We told her everything, and she agreed to gather a small crew of Avalon's most powerful witches to send to the crossroads.

Then, the Queen of Swords and I went to see her mother.

Skylar Danvers, the prophetess of Avalon, lived in beautiful quarters in one of the front turrets of the castle. Her windows overlooked the bright green mountains and sparkling blue lakes that made up the island.

Her hair was the same vibrant red as the Queen of

Swords', although her face was softer and kinder. There was a contemplative look to her eyes that made her seem like she saw and knew more than the rest of us. And she gave off the metallic scent of vampire.

That was why she had her gift of being able to see into the future. As a human, she'd been naturally gifted with reading tarot cards. After being turned into a vampire, her ability was amplified.

"Take a seat." She motioned to the table in front of the fireplace. "I'll bring over some water and mana."

Once she returned, I bit into my mana and smiled at the taste of my favorite food. Domino's pizza, with extra cheese and extra sauce. My mom and I ordered pizza every Friday night when I came home for the weekend.

The prophetess walked over to the fireplace, took a quartz crystal off the tarot deck on the mantle, and brought the deck back to the table. "I didn't know the two of you were friends," she said, looking back and forth between me and the Queen of Swords. "I assume you're coming to me with a question."

"You're a prophetess," I said. "Shouldn't you know that already?"

"You're a spunky one." The prophetess laughed, the crinkles deepening in the corners of her eyes. "You remind me of Raven."

"Thanks." It was jolting to hear so many people call the Queen of Swords by her first name. But she'd asked me to call her Raven, so I needed to force myself to think of her that way, too.

"I only see the answers to questions when I look into the cards." She removed the tarot cards from their box and placed them facedown on the table. "I didn't know you were coming because I didn't know to ask. That's the trickiest thing about seeing into the cards. Knowing what to ask."

"We already know what to ask," I said. "We need to know how to get to the Otherworld."

She held my gaze for a few seconds, and I worried she was going to tell me she couldn't do it. "I can certainly do my best to help you," she said, picking up the tarot deck and handing it to me. "Take the cards and shuffle them, thinking about your question. Once the shuffling feels complete, hand them back to me."

I did as she'd asked. It didn't take long before a warm tingle ran from my palms and up my arms.

The deck was ready. I handed it back to the prophetess.

"What did you ask the cards?" she asked.

"I asked how to get to the Otherworld and help Selena."

She nodded and started shuffling the cards again.

"That's not how we learned to do tarot readings at Avalon Academy." I pressed my lips together immediately after speaking, realizing too late that I'd probably crossed a line. It technically wasn't my place to question the prophetess. But I'd never cared about technicalities. And besides, I *did* want to know why she was using the cards that way. So I didn't apologize for misspeaking.

The prophetess continued to shuffle, looking unfazed by my curiosity. "You learned that you're supposed to shuffle, then either I'd pick the cards from the top, or you'd pick them from a fan," she said.

"Yes." I nodded.

"That's the traditional way to do a reading." She stopped shuffling the cards, and she laid them out in a fan in front of her. "This is my way. Pick a card."

I hovered my hand over the cards, waiting for one to stand out to me. When I got the same warm tingle in my hand that I'd had while shuffling, I removed the card and placed it on the table between us.

The Four of Wands.

The artwork on the card showed a man standing next to a woman on a white horse. In front of them were four tall, flaming wands.

The prophetess stared at the card intensely. It was kind of eerie. Like she was in another place, seeing something we couldn't.

Finally she looked up from the card. "The future is never set in stone," she said. "But there's a possibility that you'll be able to find your way to the Otherworld. And to do it, you'll need the help of three others who live on Avalon."

10

TORRENCE

AN HOUR LATER, I was gathered around the fireplace in the Earth Angel's quarters with the Earth Angel, the prophetess, Raven, and the three others the prophetess had seen in the tarot card.

Closest to me was Sage Montgomery, the wolf/vampire hybrid who was the alpha of the Montgomery pack. She wore all black, and her long hair was so dark that it nearly matched her outfit.

Next to her on the sofa was Thomas Bettencourt, the vampire/wolf hybrid who was gifted with power over technology. He was Sage's mate, which was why they were both hybrids. He wore a tailored suit—he looked more like a high-powered businessman than a warrior. But I knew he could fight, because both he and Sage were legends on the island, too.

In the armchair farthest away from me was Reed Holloway. He was the only male mage on Avalon, and he was the younger brother of Dahlia, Violet, and Iris. But unlike his sisters, he'd stopped wearing the medieval style clothing from the mage realm of Mystica once he got to Avalon. Probably because with his jet black hair and intense jungle green eyes, our Avalon Academy training outfits made him look even more badass than he already was.

I'd tried getting to know him when he'd come to Avalon over the summer, but he wouldn't talk to me—or any other witches at the academy. All we knew about him was that he was devoted to a princess back on Mystica. He wouldn't say anything about her, but since he didn't even *look* at any of the girls at Avalon Academy, I guessed she was really something special.

His loss. I wasn't into the broody, silent type, anyway.

The Earth Angel filled them in on what was going on with Selena. Then the prophetess told them about their appearance in her tarot reading, and how the four of us needed to work together to find an entrance to the Otherworld.

"You know I'm down," Sage said, her eyes sharpening at the mention of adventure.

"Same here," Thomas said. "But the quest would be more efficient if we knew where to start looking."

"I can try asking the cards." Skylar took them out, shuffled, and laid them out on the coffee table. She picked one and laid it flat.

The High Priestess. A dark-haired, winged woman in a blue dress, with butterflies flying around her.

The prophetess stared at the card, lost in deep concentration. The rest of us were silent as we waited for her to finish. The only sounds in the room were the flames crackling in the fireplace.

Finally, the prophetess looked up from the card. "One of the most powerful witches in the world can lead you toward the answer you seek," she said. "Unfortunately, I can't see *which* witch that is. All I know is that she doesn't live on Avalon."

"So that leaves the entire world for us to search." Sage held her head high, not looking intimidated in the slightest. "Great. We're on it."

"Not necessarily the entire world." From the level way Thomas spoke, he was clearly the calm that balanced Sage's fire. "There are a handful of places in the world where almost all of the most powerful witches reside."

"The vampire kingdoms," I blurted out.

"Yes." He nodded. "The most logical way to go about this is to ask around the vampire kingdoms and see what we can find out. We already know the Vale doesn't have any information about the Otherworld, since they're our closest ally and we spoke with them yesterday. Which means we should visit the five other kingdoms first."

"I thought you spoke with all of your allies," Reed finally added something to the conversation. "Aren't you allied with all six kingdoms?"

"We are," the Earth Angel said. "And we did send Bella and Jacen to speak with them. But Skylar said this quest was for the four of you. Perhaps you'll discover something that Jacen and Bella couldn't."

"We will." I sat forward, glad to have something important to do. "Which kingdom should we visit first?"

"We'll start with the safest one—the Haven—and continue on from there," Thomas said. "We'll save the most dangerous ones for last."

With the decision made, the Earth Angel outfitted us with holy weapons—in case we ran into any demons on our journey. Then it was time to head out.

Reed barely said a word the entire time. He technically hadn't even agreed to come on the mission. I just assumed he was coming because he hadn't said he wasn't, and because he'd taken a sword like the rest of us.

When I took Sage's hands, Reed took Thomas's, and we teleported to the vampire kingdom of the Haven.

11

TORRENCE

I'D BEEN to the Haven before. All witches on Avalon had been to the rendezvous locations for all the vampire kingdoms, so we could successfully teleport to each one of them.

The Haven was located in the lush southwestern Ghats mountain range in India, and it was positively beautiful.

We arrived right outside of the boundary. Two tigers and one girl who looked to be a few years older than me waited inside, directly across from us. She wore the white flowing pants and matching top donned by all residents of the Haven.

Because of the boundary, I couldn't smell what type of supernatural she was.

"Welcome to the Haven," she said with a warm smile. "I'm Leena. How may I help you today?"

Thomas stepped forward. "I'm Thomas Bettencourt," he said. "I'm a friend of your leader, Mary, as is my mate, Sage Montgomery. My companions and I are here on a mission from the Earth Angel, and require an immediate audience with Mary."

Before he could say any more, a woman with long brown hair riding on the back of a tiger ran to meet us. Mary. She was yet *another* legend in supernatural history. We learned all about her at Avalon Academy.

"The Earth Angel sent a message that you'd be arriving," she said, as four witches in Haven whites teleported beside us. "We'll bring you in, confirm your identities, and then we'll sit down for a chat."

———

The witches brought us to a secure room in the main building, where they took our blood to make sure we weren't demons who'd taken transformation potion to breech the kingdom.

Once our identities were confirmed, they led us to a colorful tearoom. Mary waited there with drinks and plates featuring an array of small bites. There was jasmine tea for me and Reed, and animal blood for Thomas, Sage, and Mary.

"Come, sit." Mary motioned to the red patterned cushions around the short table. "Tell me what you need."

We removed our shoes, placed them next to hers near the door, and sat down on the pillows. It was far more comfortable than it looked, although Thomas looked pretty out of place in his fancy suit.

We quickly broke bread together—as was customary when visiting a vampire kingdom—and Reed and I introduced ourselves. Then we told Mary everything that had happened since the night Selena was kidnapped.

"We're here to see if any of your witches is the one who knows how to get to the Otherworld," I concluded.

"If one of our witches knew how to get to the Otherworld, she or he would have told me," Mary said. "And if they chose not to tell me, I can't force them. Truth potion—or any potion that makes a resident of the Haven do anything against their will—is forbidden here."

"We understand," Sage said. "In that case, we were hoping for an audience with Rosella."

The vampire seer Rosella was another legend. Her visions had helped lead the Earth Angel and the Queen of Swords on their paths so they could become who they were today. I couldn't believe I'd be meeting her, too.

"I'm afraid Rosella isn't here right now," Mary said.

"When will she be back?" Sage asked.

"I can't say. Rosella often disappears for days at a time to help supernaturals in need of her guidance. You must remember that, from when she first appeared to your friend Raven."

"Is there any way you can reach her?" I asked. "We only need a few minutes of her time."

"I'm afraid not," Mary said sympathetically.

"She has to have a cell phone. Or one of your witches can send her a fire message. Please?"

"If Rosella needed to be here right now, she'd be here," Mary said. "I'm afraid you'll have to look elsewhere."

Thomas placed his teacup of blood down on the table. "Thank you for your time," he said. "Now, I don't mean to be rude and cut this short, but we need to decide which kingdom we're visiting next."

"I understand." Mary stood up, and the rest of us did the same. "I wish you luck on your mission, and I'll be praying for Selena's safe return to Avalon."

SELENA

ON THE NIGHT of the Selection Ceremony, the fireplace in my suite flared, and Vesta stepped out of the flames. She wore the same orange gown as the first day I'd met her. Apparently, that was her uniform during the Games.

"Selena," she greeted me. "I hope the past few days have been treating you well."

"They've been challenging," I said, since it was the truth.

Vesta nodded, since as the goddess of the home, she saw everything that happened in the villa. "I'll be helping you get ready, and instructing you on what you'll be doing during the ceremony," she said. "The dress your stylist sent over is stunning. He has exquisite taste."

She waved a hand at the two golden orbs in my

room, orange magic releasing from her palm and toward them. Her magic surrounded the orbs, and they both zoomed out through the door.

"We can't have anyone watching you get ready," she said with a warm smile. "That would ruin the surprise."

I didn't smile in return. Vesta was one of the gods, and no matter how caring she seemed, she was no better than the rest of them.

Then I remembered Bryan's warning about not getting on the bad sides of the gods. If the gods liked me, they'd be more likely to create competitions in my favor.

So I forced my lips up into a small smile, hoping it was convincing enough. "We wouldn't want that," I managed to say, trembling as I spoke.

But I took a deep breath, steadying myself. I couldn't afford to show any weaknesses. Not to Vesta, not to the other players, and not to the citizens of the Otherworld watching through the orbs.

Staying in control was what would keep me alive.

"No," she agreed. "We certainly wouldn't."

With the initial pleasantries over, she walked over to my wardrobe and opened both doors at once. As expected, my gown was light blue. That was my color for the Games, since it was the color of my wings. She removed it from the wardrobe and helped me put it on.

Roman in style, the dress had a tight strapless bodice

with a line of gold down the center. The skirt flowed to the floor, although there was a slit cut up to above my knee. The "sleeves" were put on separately, as they were light blue pieces of lace that started below my shoulders and ended above my elbows. Sheer fabric that matched the skirt flowed out from the end of the sleeves as well, so long that they touched the floor.

The sleeves covered the fake red tattoo that circled my right bicep. All half-bloods were given the tattoo at birth, with enchanted ink that bound their magic. It was apparently an excruciating process. Since I wasn't born with any magic, my "tattoo" was an illusion so the fae wouldn't view me as a threat.

Next, Vesta helped me accessorize. She placed thick gold cuffs around my wrists, a necklace to cover my bare chest, and earrings that dangled to my shoulders.

The entire time, she told me what to do during the ceremony. I was glad that all I had to do was listen. Because inside, my lungs were tight, my body numb. I was too anxious to talk, let alone form a complete sentence.

"Now, for the final touch," she said, placing the golden empress wreath on my head. "Take a look."

She took my hand and walked me over to the full-length mirror.

I stared at my reflection, my chest hollow. I barely

recognized myself. The outfit was fit for an empress—or a goddess.

I looked like someone who was confident and in control.

Someone who was ready to announce the three champions I'd be sending to the arena to fight to the death.

———

Vesta led the way to the library, where the ten other champions waited on the sofas and chairs surrounding the fireplace. They were all dressed in their semi-formal training gear, so I stood out in my long gown. All the orbs in the villa were in the library, too. There must have been forty or fifty of them in all.

Vesta motioned for me to enter first. When I did, a few orbs zoomed over to buzz around me, and everyone turned to look at me.

My eyes met Julian's first. He took a sharp breath inward, as if the sight of me left him breathless.

It was the same way I felt every time I looked at him.

My cheeks heated, and everyone else blurred into the background. I was trapped in his ice-blue gaze. Every bone in my body urged me to go to him.

But, of course, I held back.

He'd lied to me, kidnapped me to the Otherworld, and sold me to Prince Devyn for money, I reminded myself. *He feels nothing for me. It's all an act so he can try to wrap me around his finger, just like Felix intends to do to every female in the villa.*

Why couldn't I just hate him, like anyone else would in the same circumstance?

I didn't know, and that was a question for another time. Because I had a ceremony to lead.

I forced my eyes away from Julian's. I'd only been looking at him for two or three seconds, but it felt like my emotions were on display for everyone to see.

Hopefully no one had noticed.

Vesta walked—no, *glided*—over to the fireplace and faced all ten players. She was the total opposite of Bacchus. The calm to balance his chaos.

I followed in Vesta's wake and stood slightly off to the side, like she'd instructed me to do. I made sure to remain focused on her. I didn't want to risk accidentally staring at Julian again.

She smiled at the golden orbs floating right behind the champions. "I'm Vesta, the goddess of the hearth and the home. Welcome to the first Selection Ceremony," she said, clearly speaking to the viewers watching through the orbs and not to us. "Selena Pearce—the chosen champion of Jupiter—won the Empress of the

Villa competition for the week. Now, it's her job to select the three players she's sending to the arena to fight for their lives. Two will come out victorious and will return to the villa to continue playing in the Games. The other will move on to the Underworld, where he or she will live on for eternity in Elysium alongside other heroes and mortals related to the gods."

My insides churned at the reminder that everyone in the Otherworld believed the chosen champions were given an automatic spot in Elysium—the paradise of the Underworld. Maybe the gods were telling the truth about that, or maybe they weren't. I didn't know. It didn't matter. Because even if they were being truthful, the life we lived before passing on was meaningful and important. It shouldn't be cut short—especially in the name of a twisted form of entertainment.

Octavia, Cillian, Emmet, Pierce, and Cassia sat straighter at the mention of their destiny in the Underworld. Julian's eyes went as hard as steel. The others remained blank, impossible to read.

The ones who looked less than enthused were probably playing in the Games because of the generous lifetime stipend that would be given to their families in their honor.

Vesta aimed her orange magic toward three of the

orbs off to the side. She brought them forward to float in front of her, right below chest level.

"Selena will now take my place in the front of the library," she said. "Where she'll perform her duty as Empress of the Week and announce the three champions she's sending to the arena."

70

13

SELENA

VESTA MOVED ASIDE, and I took her place at the front of the library. As I walked, I didn't feel like I was actually there. All I saw were the three golden orbs floating in front of me. Everything else blurred into the background. My mind drew a blank.

"Selena," Vesta said with a hint of warning in her tone. "Please go ahead and announce your selections."

"Right." I cleared my throat, remembering her instructions from earlier. I looked around at the other players, trying not to pause when I got to the three I'd chosen. "This decision hasn't been easy," I started. "It's the hardest decision I've had to make in my life. But as Empress of the Week, I have no choice but to send three of you to the arena." I stared extra hard at the orbs recording me, speaking straight to the viewers.

I hoped they got the message that this wasn't something I *wanted* to do.

This was something I *had* to do to make it through this ceremony alive.

"I'll touch each orb and toss it into the air," I said. "The face of the selected champion will appear in the orb, locking in the decision of who I'll be sending to the arena."

A few of them shifted uncomfortably on the sofa. But I kept my gaze on the orbs. I didn't want anything to change my mind.

I reached forward and grabbed the first orb by the bottom. It hummed pleasantly in my hand. I thought the name of the champion I was selecting first and tossed the orb into the air.

Octavia scoffed from her seat on the sofa. "No surprise there." She smirked and squared her shoulders, looking as confident as ever.

Even though Octavia knew why I'd selected her, I was required to give my explanation to the viewers.

"Octavia, chosen champion of Neptune," I said, looking straight at her. "I've selected you because you told me during the welcome feast that you were coming for me. Since I'm the first Empress of the Villa, it only makes sense for me to come for you first."

She nodded, apparently respecting my decision. "Bring it on," she said, zeroing in on me like a cobra preparing to pounce. "I'm ready. And once I'm back in the villa, I'll be sure to stick to that promise I made you."

I didn't flinch, since she was clueless about what I'd been planning for the past few days. Her threat was an empty one.

She was in for a massive surprise in the arena.

Moving on, I reached for the second orb floating in front of me. When I tossed it in the air, Emmet's face appeared in the center.

Emmet smiled, turned to Pierce, and gave him a high five. Bridget was right—Emmet loved the attention.

"Emmet, chosen champion of Mercury," I said. "I've selected you because after I dealt the final blow against you in the fight for the horse in the Emperor Competition, you have every reason to be gunning for me. Also, you're an excellent fighter. I'm looking forward to seeing you battle it out in the arena."

"Yeah, I am!" He puffed his chest out and gave Pierce another high five.

Octavia rolled her eyes, not looking worried in the slightest.

It took all of my effort not to roll my eyes, too. Instead, I reached for the final orb. "This last decision was the hardest one to make," I said, and then I tossed it above my head.

The face of the selected champion appeared in the orb.

There was a collective sound of shock from the other champions—especially from the one I'd selected.

She was playing along well.

"Molly, chosen champion of Diana." I turned to the small girl sitting on one of the armchairs at the end of the semi-circle. My chest was hollow with guilt, even though Molly knew this was coming. "Someone else has to go to the arena with Octavia and Emmet. Your ability to shift into any animal you've touched since being gifted with your magic is impressive, as you demonstrated in the first Emperor of the Villa competition. Also, you made no effort to talk with me about the game this week. I have no idea where you stand. So unfortunately, you're the third champion I'm sending to the arena."

She simply nodded, accepting my reasoning.

"That's a lie." Octavia sat back and crossed her arms, smiling at me smugly. "You and Molly *did* talk this week. I saw you coming out of the lounge together."

"Yes, we talked." I didn't miss a beat. "But not about the Games."

Another lie. So much for trying to get through the majority of the Games without lying. But I was doing what I had to do. If that meant lying to knock Octavia out of the Games, then so be it.

Vesta walked over to stand next to me and looked at each of the players. I did the same.

I'd avoided meeting Julian, Cassia, and Bridget's gazes as I'd announced my selections. Now that I was seeing them, it was clear from their scowls and frowns that they weren't pleased with my decision. My stomach dropped, and I looked away from them, focusing on the orbs in the back of the room again.

I was going to have a *lot* of explaining to do later.

"Does anyone else have anything they wish to say?" Vesta asked.

People shifted around again, but no one else said a word.

"Then this Selection Ceremony has come to a close." Vesta aimed her orange magic at the three orbs above our heads, and they floated on top of the fireplace mantle. The three faces of the selected champions remained on the orbs, where they'd be until the end of the week.

It was a reminder to everyone in the villa—and everyone in the Otherworld—about who I'd selected.

"The three selected champions will remain in the villa until we all go to the arena," Vesta continued, giving all of us—and the orbs recording us—her familiar warm smile. "I wish all three of you the best of luck!"

14

SELENA

I HURRIED to my suite after the Selection Ceremony ended, making the excuse that I was going to change into more comfortable clothes.

It wasn't a lie. The gown felt suffocating, and all the gold jewelry I was wearing felt like lead weights bringing me down. I needed to take them *off*.

Molly came up about fifteen minutes later. Emmet came up fifteen minutes after that, sending Molly back down.

To everyone else, they were coming up to speak with me regarding my selections. It would have looked suspicious otherwise.

Only the three of us knew that everything was going according to plan.

I was still chatting with Emmet when there was a

knock on the door. I walked over to look through the peephole.

Julian was out in the hall. He stood straight as a board, his eyes focused into the door so intensely that he could have been shooting laser beams at it. I half expected him to smash it open to force his way inside.

"It's Julian," I told Emmet. "He looks *pissed*."

"Let him in," Emmet said. "Your jealous boyfriend is a good reason for me to go back downstairs."

Irritation coursed through me. Emmet was clearly trying to get a rise out of me—and it was working. "Julian's *not* my boyfriend."

"Coulda fooled me." Emmet jumped off the sofa and opened the door. "Hey there," he said to Julian, sounding as relaxed as ever. "Good timing. I was just leaving."

Julian stormed inside, not bothering to reply. He watched Emmet stroll out of the suite, spinning around to face me once the door was closed.

He didn't sit down. He just stood there in the center of the room, glaring at me.

My heart pounded faster, and I nearly stopped breathing. I'd expected Julian to be mad that I hadn't kept him and Cassia in the loop. But it was different now that I was facing the consequences of my actions. I hadn't realized I'd feel so guilty at the sight of how betrayed he looked.

"What was that about?" His voice was measured and calm. Too calm. Like he was about to explode at any second.

I wanted to go to him. I wanted to touch him and do my best to calm him down, so he'd stop looking at me with so much disappointment.

But I stayed put. Because as much as my body felt otherwise, Julian wasn't mine to touch. He never *would* be mine. I needed to accept that. So I took a deep breath to quell the sparks of magic that always flared up in his presence, until they dulled to embers under my skin.

"Do you want to sit down?" I motioned to the sofa and chairs surrounding the coffee table.

"No."

Okay, then. If he was going to stand, then I was going to remain standing, too.

He stayed like that for a few more seconds, like he was reining in all the control he could. "Me, you, and Cassia are a team," he finally said. "Bridget, too—at least for the next two weeks. We all sat up here figuring out the best strategy for making sure Octavia would be the one to go. Then you turn around and select *Molly* as the third champion, without even talking to us about it? I don't get it."

"Yes, I chose Molly," I said, refusing to show weakness by looking away. "I lied when I said we didn't discuss the Games when we were hanging out in the lounge."

"I figured as much," he said. "Octavia did, too, judging by her comment during the Selection Ceremony." Some of the tension left his body, and he walked over to sit on the sofa.

I did the same, sitting down next to him. It felt so *natural* that I didn't even realize how close we were to each other until I'd sat down. Half a foot, if even. Close enough that my wings brushed his steel gray ones and electricity buzzed through my body.

From the way he froze when I sat down, he either felt it too, or was annoyed that I was sitting so close to him. Probably the latter.

Crap. That was a mistake.

But I couldn't switch seats now. At least not without making things more awkward than they already were.

I needed to act unfazed.

So I leaned back in the sofa and crossed my legs away from his, so our wings were no longer touching. "You wanted me to send Felix to the arena," I said. "Bridget wanted me to send Pierce—"

"Pierce?" Julian interrupted, his eyes wide. "That's idiotic. Pierce isn't a meathead like Emmet. Pierce is the sort of guy who holds a grudge. Sending him to the arena would almost be as dangerous as sending Cillian. He'd come after you. No question about it."

"I know," I said. "I think Bridget was only looking out for herself with that suggestion. I trust her to keep her end of the deal we made, but that doesn't mean she's truly on our side. She was trying to get me to send Pierce to the arena so he'd come after me, and she'd continue to be off of everyone's radars."

"I agree," Julian said. "Which is why Felix would have made the most sense. Especially given the way he and Cassia act around each other. Obviously, his feelings for Cassia aren't real, but he wants her trust. And she clearly likes him. You could have convinced him to work with Emmet to take out Octavia."

I worried he was right about Cassia's feelings for Felix. But that was a conversation I needed to have with *Cassia*—not with Julian.

"Except that Venus's champions are notorious for being the worst at actual *fighting*," I reminded him. "There's no reason to think Felix is an exception. Plus, Octavia likes Felix. He has no reason to want her out this early. And I highly doubt Emmet would go for the idea of pairing up with Felix to take out Octavia, especially after Felix and Octavia shared a horse in the Emperor of the Villa competition."

Julian sat perfectly still, saying nothing.

Was that his way of admitting I was right?

With things quiet between us once again, the electricity I always felt around him crackled, firing up under my skin. Felix's words from the other day echoed in my mind.

My magic would work on you unless you've met your soulmate.

My fingers instinctively brushed where my clothes covered the clover birthmark on my left hip. If I had a soulmate, his birthmark would be identical to mine, down to its exact location.

A part of me wanted to come out with it and ask Julian if he had a matching birthmark. He'd say no, and I could put the insane notion that he could be my soulmate away for good.

But if I asked, he'd know I felt something for him. Something so intense that I believed there was a chance we were *soulmates*.

I'd never be able to live down the humiliation after he told me I was wrong.

So I just sat there, watching as he processed everything I'd said.

"Fine," he eventually said. "But why Molly? Why not Antonia? She's the chosen champion of Apollo. She's an expert with a bow and arrow."

"I considered it." I automatically leaned forward

again, making every effort to stop myself from smiling because Julian had basically just admitted I was right. "But when Octavia and Antonia fought each other to get that horse in the first competition, Octavia won. Easily. And I observed their interactions when I was downstairs this week. Antonia follows Octavia around like a puppy. She wants Octavia's favor. It didn't seem likely that she'd agree to team up with Emmet to take Octavia out."

Julian didn't say I was right, but he didn't say I was wrong, either. Which I suspected was his way of saying I was right.

"Molly, on the other hand, is a lone wolf," I continued. "She wants people to work with her, but she's shy, and she's having a hard time breaking into any groups. The moment I found time alone with her and proposed the plan, she was open to considering it. Especially after I said that if she agreed to be a pawn this week, I'd do everything I could to keep her out of the arena in the weeks following this one. She agreed, as long as Emmet was on board, too. So when Emmet came up here to speak to me—which no one noticed, since everyone except for Cillian, Octavia, and Molly came up here sometime in the past few days to talk about the game—I proposed the idea. He was happy to go to the arena with Molly to take down Octavia, because it would let him show everyone in the Otherworld that he was a force to be reckoned with."

"And you did all of this without bothering to consult any of us?" Julian asked, anger flaring in his eyes.

But I noticed something else. Worry.

Was Julian worried for me?

No, I thought, shaking off the notion. He couldn't be. I had to be imagining it.

"I *did* ask all of you," I reminded him. "Cassia said she'd support whatever decision I made. You and Bridget were both adamant about what you wanted me to do. I considered your opinions. But at the end of the day, this is my week. I had to do what felt right to me."

"And that was choosing Molly."

"Yes," I said. "Emmet brought Molly up here secretly last night, when everyone was asleep. The three of us talked. They're both on board. This plan is going to work."

Somehow during the conversation, Julian and I had moved closer to each other until we were both in the center of the sofa, nearly touching. Electricity exploded under my skin. It was just like it had been the first time I'd met him, right before we'd kissed. His pupils dilated, and I could have sworn he wanted to kiss me again, just like he had at Trevi Square.

If he did, I wouldn't have the strength to pull away.

So I scooted as far from him as possible, not giving him the chance to try anything.

Julian cleared his throat, as if trying to get ahold of himself. "Emmet's a loose cannon," he said. "But for your sake, I hope this plan works."

"It will." I stared at him, trying to will him to believe it.

We remained there, eyes locked, neither of us saying a word.

A knock on the door brought me back into focus.

I got up to see who it was, relieved to have a reason to move away from Julian. Being close to him did weird things to me, and I didn't like it.

I opened the door and saw Cassia and Bridget standing outside.

Bridget was as unreadable as ever. Cassia just looked confused.

"I'm glad you're both here." I let them in and shut the door, continuing before either of them could voice their anger, disappointment, or whatever they were feeling. "I just finished telling Julian the reason for my decision. Sit down, and I'll explain everything."

15

TORRENCE

OUR NEXT DESTINATION was the kingdom of Utopia. Utopia was a hidden island off the coast of New Zealand's north island. The residents of Utopia were only women—female vampires and female witches.

The only men on the island were humans the vampires used for their blood. Unlike in some of the other vampire kingdoms, the humans on Utopia were treated kindly.

But the women of Utopia were notorious for not trusting men—especially supernatural men. So Thomas and Reed were going to remain in the Haven while Sage and I went to Utopia. And even though it went unsaid, I suspected that Thomas and Reed were going to do some more digging in the Haven to see if there was anything they could find out that would help our quest.

Mary had a witch send a fire message to the leader of Utopia—Elizabeth—to let her know we were on our way. Elizabeth replied a few minutes later, saying she looked forward to meeting us.

I took Sage's hands and blinked us out.

Two witches waited on the small island outside of Utopia's boundary. They wore clothes of animal skin, as humans had dressed back when they were hunters and gatherers. They did the obligatory blood check to confirm our identities, and then they teleported us inside the boundary.

We landed on the top of a tall, beautiful mountain. It was much larger than any mountain on Avalon. But as I gazed out at the lush landscape before me, there were no signs of living spaces. Just a beautiful waterfall crashing into a lake, sheep scattered throughout the grass, fields full of crops, and lots and lots of bushes.

I turned around, expecting to find a town, a village, or *something*.

Instead, I saw that the top of the mountain wasn't a peak at all. It was a crater.

"We're on a volcano?" I asked.

"Mount Starlight," Harper—the more talkative of the two witches—said proudly. "Our home."

"You live *in* the volcano?" Sage looked just as confused as I felt.

"Mount Starlight is dormant," Harper said. "It hasn't erupted for over four thousand years. Our ancestors discovered it when Queen Elizabeth was searching for a location for her kingdom. They used their magic to clear the magma from the chambers, and we've been safely living inside it ever since."

My eyes widened, since I never thought I'd hear magma chambers described as *safe*. I also didn't love the idea of going inside a volcano. Small spaces weren't exactly my jam.

"Come." The other witch—Alice—motioned for us to follow her to the edge of the crater. "We'll take you inside, and bring you to the queen."

There was a spell around the volcano to prevent anyone from teleporting into it. So we had to descend the old fashioned way—by an elevator-like contraption that used ropes and pulleys to bring us down. It was large enough to hold thirty or more people, so we all had lots of space.

Once we were below the crater, I realized why the volcano was called Mount Starlight. The ceilings and walls were covered in tiny white dots that glowed like stars.

"I've never seen magic like that before," I said as I looked around, admiring the sparkling lights.

"That's because it's not magic at all," Harper said. "Each of those lights is a glowworm."

"You mean they're alive?" Sage asked.

"They're bioluminescent," she said. "Which is basically a fancy way of saying they're living creatures that glow."

I continued admiring the glowworms as we were lowered into the magma chamber. Once we were what looked to be halfway down, I caught the familiar scents of vampires, witches, and humans.

Eventually the glowworms grew sparse, and the tube opened to reveal a spacious area that housed an entire village. It must have gone on for miles.

Stacks and stacks of stone houses were carved right into the rock wall. Bridges and steps crossed the abyss, providing paths to get from one area to another. And at the bottom of the chamber was a lake, so clear that I could see the colorful fish, coral, and plants inside.

Women chatted as they walked along the paths, many of them holding woven baskets of what smelled like a variety of fruits, breads, and meats. They all wore clothes of animal hides. A few of them glanced up as our elevator landed on the highest platform, but they didn't pay us much more attention than that.

I'd expected that this deep in the Earth, it would be so dark that I wouldn't be able to see my hand in front of my face. But a warm amber glow lit the kingdom from above. I looked up and saw orbs of amber colored magic floating near the ceiling, each one around thirty or so feet away from the next.

Harper's gaze went to where I was looking. "The chamber is full of miniature suns," she said. "They exist thanks to a Final Spell gifted to us by one of the original witches of Utopia. They're timed with the actual sun, so they dim at dusk and brighten at dawn. But unlike the actual sun, their light isn't harmful to vampires."

"Wow." I leaned against the rail of the pulley-elevator, taking in as much of the underground village as I could. "This is incredible. The whole kingdom... it's just —wow."

"Not many outsiders are granted permission to enter Mount Starlight," Alice said. "Whatever you're here for must be important."

"It is," Sage said, and I instantly felt guilty for enjoying myself while Selena was trapped in the Otherworld. "And as much as we'd love a tour, time is working against us on this mission. So we need to be brought to Queen Elizabeth immediately."

16

TORRENCE

THE WITCHES BROUGHT us to the deepest part of the chamber. Across a stone bridge with no railings, a stunning vampire with long brown hair in a single braid sat on a throne.

The throne was inside of the open-mouthed skull of a dragon. It sat right where the dragon's tongue would have been.

My mind spun. Dragons didn't exist.

So how did this skull get there?

The people of Utopia have built it—sculpted it somehow. Yeah. That made sense.

"Sage Montgomery and Torrence Devereux," the queen said, her voice echoing through the chamber. "Step forward."

Sage and I crossed the bridge to stand in front of the

queen. She wore many different types of animal skin layered on top of one another. On her head was a jagged crown made of bones and teeth. And most disturbingly, spherical things about the size of fists hung from her belts.

The spherical things looked like shrunken *heads*.

She must have noticed that I was staring, because she touched the top of one of the heads and stroked its hair lovingly. "The heads of my male lovers throughout the ages," she said. "I keep them by my side, so they can be with me forever."

It took every ounce of my willpower not to turn to Sage and give her a look that said we needed to get out of there, pronto.

"How thoughtful of you," Sage said, as diplomatic as ever.

I swallowed down disgust, purposefully looking the queen straight in the eyes so I wouldn't focus on the shrunken heads.

"Harper and Alice," the queen said to the two witches standing behind us. "Bring forth the bread."

Harper brought a bite-sized piece of bread to the queen, and Alice brought two similarly sized pieces to me and Sage. Once we all had our bread, the witches scurried back to their places behind us.

The queen popped her piece of bread into her mouth, chewed, and swallowed. We did the same.

She nodded in approval. "Mary said in her fire message that you needed to see me regarding an issue of great importance," she said. "While I don't know either of you, I do trust Mary. So tell me what you seek."

I'd been involved in this for longer than Sage, so I summarized everything that had happened up until now.

"We're hoping one of your witches has the information we need," Sage said once I'd finished.

The queen's gaze flickered to the witches behind us. "Alice," she said. "Step forward, face our guests, and speak your piece."

Alice walked forward to stand next to the queen's throne and turned to us. "My grandmother used to be the head witch of the Tower," she said, her eyes darkening as she spoke the name of the most lawless vampire kingdom of them all. "Her name was Donatella. She escaped here to Utopia, where she lived in peace before passing on to the Beyond. But before she passed on, she left me a message. She told me that years ago, when I was a young child, the seer of the Haven came to see her."

"Rosella," Sage said.

"Yes." Alice nodded. "Rosella told her that sometime

in the future, I'd meet a shifter/vampire hybrid and a powerful teenage witch of your descriptions, and that you'd ask me this very question. I knew it was the two of you when you teleported in, but I had to bring you here to hear the words from your mouths, just to make sure. Rosella said the fate of the world depended on top secret information my grandmother was privy to as head witch of the Tower."

"Your grandmother knew how to get to the Other-world?" I bounced on my toes, eager for Alice to be out with it so we could get on with finding Selena.

"She knew that the king of the Tower—King Devin—went to the crossroads decades ago and met a faerie princess there," she said. "He was infatuated with her. He visited her at the crossroads on every full moon for months. Eventually, they fell in love. He started to disappear for days at a time. During that time, my grandmother took advantage of his inattentiveness to the kingdom to escape. I don't know if he still visits his faerie princess. I suspect not, because the Tower has become more and more violent over the past twenty years. But if anyone might know how to get to the Otherworld, it's him."

"The king of the most lawless vampire kingdom in the world." Sage sighed. "Our alliance with the Tower is shaky, at best. Of *course* it's him."

"Important quests are rarely easy," the queen said with a twinkle in her eye. "But Rosella wouldn't have left this information for you if she didn't think you could handle it."

But visions of the future were never set in stone. The future was malleable. One bad choice, and the web could unravel, weaving into something new. Just because Rosella saw that we had a chance of pulling this off didn't mean we would.

But at least we knew we had a shot.

"Thank you, Your Highness." I bowed my head slightly to the queen. "And thank you, Alice and Harper."

"You're welcome," the queen said. "Now, get to the Tower, and figure out how to save the Earth Angel's daughter."

17

TORRENCE

I BLINKED Sage and me back to the Haven, so we could pick up the guys. Leena met us at the boundary and checked our blood again to confirm our identities.

Apparently, that hadn't been a thing before the demons broke out of Hell and came to Earth. Extra precautions had been put into place since then.

Mary escorted us back into the tearoom, where Thomas and Reed were lounging and enjoying local faire that smelled positively delicious.

The guys silenced the moment we entered.

"Well?" Reed looked doubtful that we'd been successful.

Ugh. What an arrogant prick.

"We got a lead." I smirked, glad to prove his doubts

wrong. From there, I told them what we'd learned during our visit to Utopia.

Reed looked bored, continuing to enjoy his food as I spoke.

I hated him more and more the longer I was around him.

"We have to go to the Tower and speak to King Devin," I said, turning to Mary. "Can you have a witch send him a fire message, like you did with Queen Elizabeth?"

"Many supernaturals of the Tower—especially the women—try escaping the Tower to come to the Haven," she said gently. "Some are successful. Others are not. But as you can imagine, our two kingdoms are not on good terms. Luckily, we have our tiger shifters to protect us. Without them, I suspect the Tower would have tried decimating us centuries ago."

"Oh." I deflated. "So we should just... pop in?"

"I'm afraid that sounds like as good a plan as any."

Thomas stood up, and Reed did the same—although Reed looked annoyed that he had to end his meal early. "The two of you are going to have to let Reed and me take the lead," Thomas said.

Sage crossed her arms and stared him down. "You're not going without us," she said. "This isn't Utopia we're dealing with. This is the Tower. Four of us are stronger than two. We need as much manpower as possible."

"I never said we were going without you," Thomas said. "But you know how King Devin is."

"Not firsthand." Sage scowled. "I'd never dream of entering that place."

"I'm guessing King Devin is as much of a sexist pig as they say," I said.

"He is." Thomas nodded. "He's almost as conniving as the fae. The best way to efficiently get the information we need is to play by his rules." He looked at Sage when he said that, since she was the Montgomery alpha. Sitting back was *not* natural for any alpha.

"We can do it," I said firmly. "For Selena."

"Yes." Sage gave a pained smile. "For Selena, for the Earth Angel, and for everyone else on Avalon."

18

SELENA

VESTA WALKED me down to the foyer on the morning of the arena fight, where the other champions were already waiting. I was in a gown similar to the one I'd worn during the Selection Ceremony, and the golden wreath was on my head.

Octavia, Emmet, and Molly all wore golden gladiator outfits. Neither the female nor the male outfits left much to the imagination.

Emmet's chest was bare, and a gladiator bottom hung from his waist. He had a chain crossing his chest and golden bands around his wrists, but that was it.

Octavia and Molly had similar bottoms as Emmet. Their tight tops exposed their stomachs and pushed up their breasts. They also wore the golden chains around their wrists. And all three of them wore flat gladiator sandals tied up to their knees.

In the movies from Earth that I'd watched on Avalon, it was a common joke that humans used Halloween as an excuse to wear an outfit too sexy for everyday life. These gladiator costumes reminded me of that.

Molly stood off to the side. She chewed on her lower lip, her face whiter than I'd ever seen it.

I walked over to her and took her hands in mine. She was trembling. "You've got this," I said, speaking softly to avoid bringing attention to us.

"I know." She glanced toward the doors, then back at me. "It just all feels so real now."

"It's going to be okay." I couldn't bring up our deal with everyone there, but she had to understand my reminder that the plan was good to go.

Just to be safe, I glanced at Emmet. He winked at me and Molly, as confident as ever. I squeezed Molly's hands, as if saying, *See? It'll be fine.*

She relaxed slightly, even managing a small smile.

"Comforting a champion you sent to the arena?" Octavia's haughty voice filled the foyer. "How sweet of you."

I dropped Molly's hands and turned to face Octavia. Her ocean blue gaze was as fierce as ever.

"I didn't realize you needed comforting," I said. "All you needed to do was ask."

The orbs circled excitedly above our heads. Interactions between Octavia and me seemed to be their favorite.

"Oh, I don't." She smirked. "And you should stop looking at me like I'm dead already. Because I'm going to survive. And then, I'm going to make the Games your own personal nightmare."

———

Vesta sent us off in glass carriages like the one Cinderella took to the ball. Like Prince Devyn's carriages, ours were pulled by winged horses.

I had a carriage to myself. The champions heading to the arena had one for the three of them. The others split off into groups. The golden orbs followed us into our carriages, as intent as ever to record our every move.

Julian sat with Bridget, which didn't bother me. Bridget was all business when it came to the Games. I assumed they were using the time together to strategize.

Cassia shared a carriage with Felix. Octavia's eyes narrowed as she watched Felix help Cassia up into the carriage, her upper lip curving up into a snarl.

At least Octavia wouldn't be here after this week to

set her sights on Cassia, too. Although I tried not to think about it, since "not being here" meant she'd be dead.

My chest tightened at the reminder. Because as much as I hated Octavia, I didn't want her dead. I didn't want *any* of the other champions dead.

The only thing keeping me sane was knowing that my father was coming with the Nephilim army to put a stop to this madness.

I just had to stay alive until he did.

The half-blood flying my carriage gave me a respectful nod, although he didn't acknowledge me after that. He couldn't, since the public wasn't allowed to interfere with the Games. The gods had put a spell on everyone living in the Otherworld to ensure it. Which meant I rode the entire way to the city in silence.

After about an hour, the stone, Roman-style build-ings with vines and flowers curling around them grew denser. I leaned forward and pressed my hand against the glass, watching as we approached the capital. Despite being a prisoner in the Otherworld, I couldn't deny that the realm was beautiful.

If things had been different, I might have loved it. But after what I'd been through, it would be forever tainted.

Eventually, we descended toward the building that

I'd recognize anywhere—the Coliseum. But other than its shape, this Coliseum was nothing like the one in my Ancient History 101 textbook. It was bright white marble, and like every other building in the Otherworld, green, flowery vines wrapped around its many columns and arches. A gold awning covered the top of the building nearly to the center, blocking me from seeing inside.

Faeries and half-bloods alike were packed on the streets, in line to enter the giant building.

Once we were flying about twelve feet over the ground, my carriage and the carriages holding the majority of the champions turned left around the arena. The one with the three players I'd selected to send to the arena turned right.

We landed on a wooden dock above the crowds, on the second floor of the arena. A beautiful faerie woman waited for us.

She had long platinum hair similar to my own, although the pointed tips of her ears stuck out beneath it. Her eyes were somehow every shade of blue at once. She wore a white floor-length dress embellished with pearls, the fronts of her glass heels peeking out from the bottom. A pearl crown that must have been a foot tall rested on her head, and her wings sparkled like diamonds. No other faerie had wings like those.

Despite being petite, she had a presence that would make anyone fall to their knees.

The Empress of the Otherworld. Sorcha.

She waited with her hands clasped in front of her as we exited our carriages and lined up to face her.

As Empress of the Villa, I took my spot in the center of the semi-circle.

Compared to Sorcha's stunning pearl crown, my Empress of the Villa wreath looked like a joke. A mockery of power.

That was exactly what it was meant to be. But I held my head high, not wanting to appear intimidated. Intimidation would be taken as weakness. And I couldn't afford to look weak.

Once we were lined up, our carriages flew off, leaving us alone with the empress.

A group of fae gathered below the dock. They looked up at us and pointed like we were celebrities.

"Welcome to the Coliseum." Sorcha gave us a pleasant, closed-lip smile. "And congratulations, Selena, for winning the first Emperor of the Villa competition."

I nearly said thank you, but caught myself before I did. Thanking a fae was the equivalent of owing them a debt. I needed to be careful with my words.

"I did my best." I lowered my eyes slightly, not wanting to say or do anything that might anger the empress. That would be nearly as bad as angering the gods.

"You did well," she said, and I lifted my gaze to meet hers again. If she felt anything other than serenity and peace, I never would have known.

"I'm honored that you think so."

Apparently satisfied with my response, she gave me a slight nod and turned her focus back to the group. "This dock leads straight to the Royal Box, to keep you separated from the public during the fight," she said, motioning to the double doors behind her. Her voice was like music, somehow managing to be authoritative, calm, and soothing all at once. "Follow me inside, but remain in the back of the box. Once I'm standing in front of my throne, proceed forward to stand in front of your seats. As Empress of the Week, Selena will take the smaller throne next to mine. I'll sit, you'll sit, and then, the arena battle will begin."

19

SELENA

THE MOMENT SORCHA entered the Royal Box, everyone in the arena silenced and stood up. The inside of the arena smelled strangely sweet, like honey and roses.

From where I stood in the back of the box, I could only see the people sitting in the upper bleachers. They were all half-bloods. Of course the half-bloods had the worst seats in the house. They looked like dots in a swarm of ants.

My stomach swooped as it set in that we were about to be on display in front of so many people. It was one thing knowing they were watching through the orbs. It was far more real to see them in person.

"How many people fit in the arena?" I asked Cassia, who was standing next to me.

Bridget piped in before Cassia could answer. "Fifty

to eighty thousand," she said. "For the Games, it's filled to maximum capacity."

I took a sharp breath inward, my heart pounding faster. That was more than ten times the amount of people that lived on Avalon. I'd never seen that many people congregated in one place in my life.

Sorcha glided to her throne—a sparkling chair made of pure crystal. The light gleamed off every angle of it, and spikes shot out from the top like the rays of the sun.

Once she turned to face the crowd, I walked toward the far less impressive golden throne beside hers. As I continued forward, I saw more and more of the interior of the Coliseum.

All of the seats were marble. As expected, the fae had the best seats, lower down and closer to the action. People held onto a variety of snacks—cakes, fruits, and sweetmeats—although they'd all stopped eating when Sorcha had entered.

Then the center of the Coliseum came into view, and I stopped in my tracks.

The bottom of the arena was filled with water. Tons of tons of water, so dark that it looked like it had been ripped out of the middle of the ocean.

Three Roman warships floated in the center. Made of wood, the sides of the ships were painted three different colors. Ocean blue, pure white, and deep violet. The wing colors of Octavia, Emmet, and Molly, in that order.

A golden trident sat on the hull of each ship.

There was only one reason to design this fight with water and tridents.

The gods—and the fae—must want Octavia to win.

"Selena?" Sorcha said, and I blinked a few times, remembering that tens of thousands of people were watching us. "Come take your place next to me."

It's okay, I told myself as I walked toward the Empress of the Villa throne. *Emmet and Molly are on board with the plan. They're strong fighters. They can beat Octavia, even while she's surrounded by her element. And Emmet's element is air. Along with being surrounded by water, they're surrounded with air, too. They've got this.*

I reached the throne and turned to face the crowd. But I barely saw any of the people inside the Coliseum. All I could focus on was the watery battlefield.

The other players walked to their seats after us. Their marble chairs were a step below and in front of our thrones. As instructed, they remained standing in front of their seats.

Sorcha took her time gazing around the entirety of the arena. No one spoke as she studied them. It was so quiet that I was afraid to breathe. Finally, she looked straight ahead again and lowered herself onto her throne.

I sat down next, followed by the other players, followed by the fae, and lastly, by the half-bloods. Once seated, everyone remained quiet. It was a massive change from their raucous behavior in front of the gods.

Servants entered the Royal Box—one servant for each of us—and presented us with trays of snacks and honeyed wine.

Sorcha took a pastry with apricot jam in the center and a glass of wine.

I needed to keep my head clear during the Games, so I passed on the wine. But not wanting to get on the bad sides of the fae or the gods, I took a date and popped it in my mouth.

Since the arena was still silent, I gave the servant a small smile and a nod, hoping to convey that the date was all I wanted. He bowed his head and hurried with the other servants to stand in the back of the box.

I looked around for Prince Devyn, assuming he'd have one of the best seats in the house. But the crowd was so huge that I couldn't spot him.

Maybe he was watching through the orbs.

Or maybe he wasn't watching at all, because his omniscient sight had already told him what was going to happen.

Suddenly, there was an explosion of bright light at the top center of the arena. Bacchus rode out of it, like he was coming through a curtain.

Four black panthers pulled his chariot. He held his pinecone scepter, although now he wore a black toga that covered only his bottom. His chiseled chest was bare—minus the snake curled around his neck. His eyes gleamed with a bloodthirsty madness they hadn't had before.

The crowd stood and stomped their feet, getting louder and louder until the noise rumbled in my chest. This was the crowd I remembered. But their cheers were darker now. Twisted. Yearning for blood.

Sorcha remained calm and unmoving in her throne. It was impossible to tell whether she supported the Faerie Games or not.

Bacchus circled the arena a few times, the eyes of his panthers glowing bright yellow. His dark gaze met mine, and shivers traveled up and down my spine.

Finally he settled down, his chariot floating in the center of the arena. His panthers sat down on what was seemingly empty space. One of them started licking its paw.

Bacchus raised his scepter, and the crowd quieted. "Citizens of the Otherworld!" he said, his voice booming through the amphitheater. "You've come from near and far to watch the first fight to the death of this year's Faerie Games. We've gone all out for you, to give you a show you'll never forget. Doesn't the arena look spectacular?!"

He motioned to the water below him, and the crowd went wild again. They didn't stop until he raised his scepter once more.

"I'm sure you all know the rules, but since it's the first fight of the Games, it's my duty to remind you of them," he continued. "When I give the go, the three champions selected by this week's Empress of the Villa will enter the arena."

All eyes in the stadium went to me, and Bacchus grinned wickedly.

I clenched my fists where they rested on the armrests. Electricity sparked below my skin, and my hands lit up with it, orbs of lightning surrounding them.

The crowd cheered again. The orbs around my hands grew, and the crowd's cries became louder and louder.

They thought I was doing this to entertain them. But as their cheers grew, so did my anger, and so did the globes of lightning around my hands. They were the size of basketballs, and getting bigger.

I needed it to *stop*.

Glancing over at Sorcha, I steadied my breathing, embracing her serene aura.

After what felt like the longest few seconds of my life, the orbs around my hands shrank until extinguishing completely.

All eyes returned to Bacchus.

"The stage is designed uniquely for each fight," the god continued. "Since these fights can get messy, there are barrier spells surrounding the perimeter of the stage for your protection. On my go, the three chosen champions will enter the arena, and will fight using their magic and the tools provided for them. They'll fight until one of them is dead. Simple enough, right?"

The crowd roared and clapped once again. It was almost like Bacchus's presence worked them into a frenzy. Only those of us inside the Royal Box appeared unaffected.

He raised his scepter and shot purple magic toward the ceiling, making the crowd burst into another wave of cheers and applause. The magic burst into a cloud cover, and bunches of grapes rained down on the audience. People reached upward to catch the grapes, shoving past each other to get to them. They cheered and raised the grapes above their heads in victory before digging in.

One of the bunches dropped straight onto my lap. It smelled of fruit and alcohol.

Bacchus had made the grapes alcoholic.

I picked up the bunch of grapes by the stem, held it out above the floor, and called upon my magic. The electricity sizzled under my skin, and I shot it into the grapes, disintegrating them in a second. The ash floated down to the floor.

No one noticed. The grapes continued to fall. Fae and half-bloods alike continued to catch them and cheer.

Anger crackled through my body. The electricity grew hotter and stronger as I watched them lower entire bunches to their mouths and devour the grapes straight from the stems, like animals.

My trainers had warned me that the Games were viewed as entertainment. They'd warned me that the competitions were rigged.

They hadn't warned me that the fights to the death would be full-blown *celebrations*.

The grapes kept coming, falling faster and faster.

I couldn't watch it anymore.

I stood up, raised my hands, and released bolts of lightning toward the grapes falling in front of the Royal Box. I struck one after another, like I was a huntress and the grapes were my prey. I didn't even pause to breathe.

My lightning kept coming, fueled by each bunch of grapes I struck down from the air. The sheer power of it was electrifying.

I didn't count how many bunches of grapes I'd turned to ash before realizing that the entire arena had gone quiet.

Bacchus lowered his scepter, his purple magic disappeared, and the grapes stopped falling. He stared me down with eyes that hungered for blood. His panthers stared at me, too. The other players had turned to watch me as well. Most of them looked entertained by my spectacle. Julian, Cassia, and Bridget were horrified.

I slowly sat back down. The electricity coursing through me fizzled out completely.

Just like with the orbs, my magic had taken control of my body. It had a mind of its own. And it didn't care if it broke the rules of the Games.

My heart pounded. I looked at Bacchus, gripping the armrests of my throne and waiting for him to call upon Juno to decide my punishment.

Bacchus threw his head back and laughed. "Jupiter's chosen champion is determined to steal the spotlight!" he said once he'd gotten ahold of himself. "That doesn't seem fair to the champions she selected to fight for their lives today, does it?"

One fae raised a bunch of grapes in the air and started chanting.

Fight! Fight! FIGHT!

Everyone joined in, repeating the word over and over and over.

Bacchus spun around in his chariot, grinning as the feverish chant grew so loud that it could probably be heard in the neighboring city.

My transgression was being celebrated—not condemned.

Confused, I thought back to the rule I'd broken when I'd destroyed the orbs.

Any player who attacks or destroys objects created by the gods for use in the Faerie Games will be punished.

Realization set in. Unlike the orbs, the grapes weren't created for *use* in the Faerie Games. They were created to add excitement.

I hadn't broken any rules. My magic had shown itself to be volatile and dangerous, which would likely put even more of a target on my back. But I'd escaped punishment thanks to simple rhetoric.

Bacchus's eyes danced with amusement, and he raised his scepter back into the air.

The crowd's sudden silence was more deafening than the chanting.

By now, I was convinced that Bacchus was affecting

the emotions of everyone in the arena. He *had* to be. There was no other explanation for the hold he had on them.

He continued looking down on the crowd, his grin morphing into something animalistic and feral. "You all came here for a fight!" he said, and the audience cheered in approval. "So it's time I gave you a fight!"

He pumped his scepter into the air again. Three doors set far away from each other at the bottom of the arena slid down, spilling more water inside.

Three people in gold gladiator costumes floated out in tiny rowboats—one from each door.

Molly, Emmet, and Octavia.

20

SELENA

EACH ROWBOAT HEADED toward one of the bigger ships in the center of the arena. It was set up so each champion could get to the ship painted the color of his or her wings, grab their trident, and fight.

Octavia raised her hands, and blue magic poured out of them, connecting with the water. It rose up like a fountain beneath her rowboat and dropped her onto the deck of her ship, where she grabbed her trident.

Molly shifted into one of her favorite forms—a hawk —and flew toward her ship.

Emmet used his magic over air to fly toward Molly's ship. He was going to help her.

But he gathered his white magic and pushed a gust of wind toward her, flinging her across the arena.

She smacked into the invisible wall surrounding the perimeter with a sickening crack and slid down into the teaming water below. Right before she hit the water, she shifted back to human form.

My breath caught in my chest. The crowd cheered, but it was muffled around me.

Emmet can't attack Molly, I thought. *This must be a ploy so Octavia doesn't realize the two of them are about to gang up against her.*

He swooped down onto Molly's ship and grabbed her trident. Then he zoomed over to his ship and grabbed his trident. He held both of them over his head in victory, setting the crowd off into a frenzy again.

Molly didn't surface from the water.

Octavia stood on the hull of her ship with her trident in hand, smirking as she watched Emmet's boastful display.

I looked desperately into the water for Molly, although the water was so dark that it was impossible to see where she was. But she was still alive. If she'd drowned, Bacchus would have already ended the fight.

Emmet flew over to Octavia's ship, landed beside her, and handed her one of his tridents. "It's only fitting for the chosen champion of Neptune to have an extra trident," he said, magic amplifying his voice so everyone in the arena could hear.

"Yes, it is." Octavia narrowed her eyes and surveyed the water. Her blue magic thrummed through the tridents and came out of their points, swirling around her. Like Emmet, her voice was also magically amplified so we could all hear. "After all, I have a fish to fry."

Her magic spread outward toward the water. The surface roughened, angry waves cresting and crashing against the sides of the arena. The ships bobbed like they were in a storm at sea.

Molly wouldn't be able to hide for much longer.

"Fight back," I said, although the claps of the crowd drowned out my cry, and Molly clearly couldn't hear me. "Come on, Molly. Fight back."

My magic crackled to life in my chest, jolts of electricity rushing through my body.

The magic didn't have time to surface before there was a light brush of fingers on my arm. Sorcha. At her touch, calmness floated through me like a shot of morphine.

Nothing you do or say can affect the fight now. The empress remained facing forward, her voice echoing in my mind. *You need to learn how to control your magic. For now, this will do the trick. But it's only temporary.*

She moved her hand away, although the calming effect she'd had on me remained. The intense electricity of my magic had dulled to a low hum.

Like all fae royalty, she was gifted.

And she was using her gift to help me.

Why was she helping me? But more importantly…

"Isn't interfering with the Games against the rules?" I asked.

"I'm the empress of the Otherworld," she said with a serene smile. "I can do whatever I want. And preventing you from having another outburst is beneficial to everyone watching the Games."

"How so?" With her magic dulling my senses and emotions, I was as cool and collected as she was. Especially since no one was paying attention to us. They were too focused on the fight in the arena.

"You're intriguing," she said simply. "It would be disappointing if Jupiter's first chosen champion did something stupid to get herself eliminated from the Games this early on. And the last thing I want is for the citizens of the Otherworld to be disappointed."

Sorcha wasn't helping me out of kindness. Of course she wasn't. She viewed us as pawns—just like the gods.

Suddenly the crowd roared, and I whipped my head back around to refocus on the center of the arena.

A great white shark as big as a school bus had burst forth from the water. Molly. She propelled herself toward Octavia, her mouth wide open, her multiple rows of sharp teeth bared.

Yes, I thought, although my emotions felt distant and dull because of whatever Sorcha had done to me. *Take her down.*

But Octavia shot a stream of water straight at Molly, knocking her back into the teaming waves. Water splashed around Molly as she crashed back down. Then Octavia hurled one of her tridents straight at the spot where Molly had just landed.

As the trident connected with the water, there was a crunching, cracking sound from the other side of the ship. The ship upended, and Octavia stumbled. Then, the ship started to sink.

Molly had bitten a hole in it.

Octavia and Emmet took a running leap off the end of their ship and jumped.

Emmet flew in an arc through the air, landing on Molly's still intact ship.

A jet of water gathered beneath Octavia, propping her up. It went up to her waist, and she was right in the center of it, like a mermaid out for blood. The trident she'd flung into the water soared out of the surface and landed back into her hand, in the same way Thor called for his hammer.

"You can't beat me in my own element!" Octavia screamed down at the water crashing below. The waves were angrier than before. If it weren't for the invisible shield around the arena, everyone on the first level would have been soaked.

She raised both tridents above her head and dove into the water.

People in the stands stood up and peered forward, as if that would help them see what was happening under the surface. But besides the occasional flash of fin or tail, we had no idea what was going on down there.

I prayed that Molly was getting the best of Octavia.

Emmet rushed to the mast of the ship and pulled at the ropes holding up the sails. He gathered the rope and flew in a circle around the mast, tugging harder and harder. Finally, he flew outward with so much speed that the end of the rope snapped and broke away from the mast completely. He dropped back onto the deck and laid the rope out by his feet, kneeling and tying it into knots.

People focused on their food and drinks, not interested in whatever task Emmet was setting out to complete.

After what felt like minutes, Octavia burst forth from a jet of water and landed next to Emmet, collapsing in a heap next to him. The bottom halves of her legs were mangled and bloodied—like they'd been munched on by a shark. Her tridents were gone.

The crowd took a collective, disappointed breath inward.

Octavia sat up, her legs too injured for her to stand. "She's too big and fast for the tridents to do enough damage." She scowled down at the water below, searching for Molly. "We need her back in her human form. Or any form smaller than that shark."

Emmet hovered behind her and raised his trident, his eyes like lasers blazing a hole into her back.

Do it, I thought, leaning forward and holding my breath. *One jab though the heart. That's all it'll take.*

I recoiled a second later. There I was, wishing for Emmet to murder Octavia. I was no better than the rest of them.

Maybe Bacchus's bloodlust was getting to me, after all. Or maybe Sorcha's calming touch had loosened my thoughts.

But Octavia had to die in the arena today. Otherwise it would be Molly. And Molly deserved to live. I wouldn't be able to forgive myself if she died.

If Emmet was going to stay true to his word and turn on Octavia, he needed to do it *now*.

But he stepped back, his posture relaxing. "I have a plan," he said.

Octavia rotated around to face him. "What kind of plan?" she asked.

He picked up the rope, held onto the end, and swung it above his head. He'd tied it into a giant lasso. "Think you can get Molly back to the surface again?"

"She got my legs—not my hands." Octavia scoffed. "I can still use my magic. Can you make the ship hover above the water?"

Emmet tossed her his trident, and she caught it easily. "You'll know when to throw it," he said.

With one hand free again, he pushed his white air magic beneath the ship and did exactly what Octavia had requested. His magic poured out in a continual stream, the air between the water and the ship sparkling white as it kept the ship hovering above the surface.

"Perfect." Octavia scooted forward and used her free hand to shoot her blue magic straight into the water in the center of the arena.

The water swirled and swirled, until it was a whirlpool going straight to the bottom. The other ship —the one painted white—was sucked into the deadly funnel, crunching and breaking until all that was left of it was debris floating on the surface.

"Fly our ship next to the whirlpool," Octavia said, screaming to be heard over the roaring water. "Molly won't be able to fight the strength of it much longer. And once we see her..." She paused, her eyes glinting with bloodlust.

"You'll bring her up, and I'll force her to shift back," Emmet said. "And we'll take her down."

21

SELENA

THE WHIRLPOOL SWIRLED STRONGER and stronger. Soon enough, Molly's shark form appeared on the edges.

"Found her." Octavia smirked.

"Bring her up," Emmet said. "Just the way you rode those jet streams earlier."

Octavia pushed out a burst of her ocean blue magic. The whirlpool slowed at the same time as a jet stream rose Molly up in the air.

Molly flipped her fins and tail, struggling to get free. But the water surrounding her was *binding* her. She could barely move.

Octavia's command over the water was stronger than any of us had realized. Yet, because of whatever Sorcha had done to me, my emotions were still muted. I *knew* Octavia's power was scary, but I couldn't *feel* the shock and the horror that I should have felt while watching her and Emmet gang up on Molly. It was like the consequences of what I was seeing hadn't sunk in. Or like the consequences didn't exist at all.

I didn't want Sorcha to touch me ever again.

Hopefully it wore off soon.

Octavia pulled the jet stream closer and closer to the ship, bringing Molly along with it. Molly bared her teeth, ready to chomp once she was close enough to reach them.

With the whirlpool gone, Emmet released his hold on the ship, lowering it until it was floating on the water again.

"Stop," Emmet said once Molly was just out of biting range.

Streams of water and blue sparkling magic circled Molly like a net, keeping her locked in place. Molly continued to struggle, but she was only wasting her energy.

Now that Molly was closer to them—and also closer to the trident—I saw what Octavia meant about the trident being too small to injure Molly in this form. It would be like trying to attack a person with tweezers. Not even, because Molly's hide looked much thicker than our skin.

"Whatever you're going to do, do it soon." Octavia's

mangled legs were losing blood quickly. She was using the handle of the trident like a stick, propping herself up so she remained sitting fully upright. "I can't hold her like this for much longer."

"On it." Emmet threw the lasso over his head and circled it around and around to gather momentum. His white air magic sparkled around the rope.

He flung the lasso forward. It wrapped perfectly around Molly's form. Just before reaching her fin, Emmet pulled tight on the lasso, locking it in place.

Molly's eyes bulged, and her struggling intensified. But she couldn't pull free of Emmet's lasso. His air magic surrounded it, holding strong.

The longer the lasso held, the more Molly struggled. The light started to go out of her eyes. She looked like she was going to go unconscious at any second.

He was suffocating her.

And I was just watching, unable to stop it. Even if Sorcha hadn't done whatever she'd done to me, there was nothing I'd be able to do. Jumping in to help Molly was against the rules. Juno would smite me on the spot. And then the Games would go on the same as always.

All I could do was pray for a miracle.

"She has to return to her human form between shifts," Emmet murmured to Octavia. "That's when you need to throw the trident. I'll make sure it hits its mark."

Molly held out for another full minute, continuing her futile attempts to break free of the rope. But then the air around her shimmered, and she shifted from shark back to human.

Octavia hurtled the trident toward Molly. And as Emmet had promised, he pushed his white wind magic behind her throw, ensuring the center point of the trident speared straight through Molly's heart.

Molly's violet wings flickered once, twice, three times. Then their light went out. There was nothing left where they'd been. They were just gone. All that remained was Molly's bleeding corpse, held up by Octavia's stream of water.

Octavia pushed out more magic and raised the stream of water higher, elevating Molly like a trophy.

The crowd exploded into cheers and chanted Octavia's name.

Octavia turned and focused on me. "You thought you could get rid of me so easily!" she screamed, the crowd quieting as her sharp words filled the arena. "But this was only a taste of what I can do. You just sealed your fate in the Games, Selena. And I hope you enjoyed seeing what's coming for you."

She dropped her hold of the jet stream, lowering Molly into the now flat surface of the water below.

Molly's body floated lifelessly, her blood seeping into the water around her like spilled ink.

A cold wave of horror sank to the marrow of my bones.

Molly's death was my fault. If I hadn't trusted Emmet's word, she'd still be alive right now.

They're all going to die sometime. The thought popped into my head—unwelcome, but true. *Maybe not today. Maybe not next week. But eventually, if I want to win the Games, every single one of them will have to die.*

Because of the serenity Sorcha had forced upon me, the reminder didn't frighten me as much as before.

But *was* it because of what Sorcha had done to me? Or was I coming to terms with the cold hard truth of what would happen if the Nephilim army didn't come for me, and I needed to win the Games?

Before I could dwell on it further, Sorcha stood from her throne, staring regally out at the crowd. Everyone else in the Coliseum followed her lead—including myself and the other players.

The golden orbs flew around Bacchus, and he raised his scepter.

"Molly—the chosen champion of Diana—is officially the first defeated champion of the Games!" he said. "Her soul is on its way to Elysium, where she'll be honored as a goddess for all eternity. May her crossing to the Underworld be a peaceful one!"

"May her crossing to the Underworld be a peaceful one!" the crowd repeated in unison, their voices echoing through the concrete arena.

Chills crept up and down my spine at the cult-like creepiness.

Bacchus waited a few seconds, and then continued, "Octavia and Emmet have proven themselves worthy of continuing to compete in this year's Faerie Games," he said. "So, as always, it's my pleasure to welcome Vejovis —the son of Apollo—into the arena to use his golden rod to heal the injuries sustained by today's victors."

I barely paid attention as the healer god used his golden rod to heal Octavia and Emmet.

Because tomorrow, there'd be a competition to crown a new Emperor of the Villa.

Cassia and Bridget were the only players I trusted to keep me safe. And Julian, as much as I hated to admit it.

One of them *had* to win.

If they didn't, I had a sinking feeling that next week, I'd be in the center of the arena fighting for my life.

TORRENCE

T<small>HE</small> T<small>OWER</small> <small>KINGDOM</small> was a gleaming collection of modern skyscrapers in the eastern section of Caracas, Venezuela. The buildings were so tall that they shot straight up into the clouds.

The skyscrapers were the only things that shined in Caracas. The rest of the bleak city consisted of nearly ruined buildings and shantytowns on the verge of collapse.

We teleported to the gate of the walled-in skyscrapers. A lineup of vampires and shifters dressed in identical soldier outfits stood in front of the arched entrance. All of the guards were male. They were armed to the teeth with longswords and daggers.

The tallest, most muscular of the vampires stood

front and center. His eyes roamed up and down Sage's body, and then moved on to mine.

His gaze felt like a snake slithering along my skin, and I shuddered in disgust.

"State your business." The guard's voice was laced with a Spanish accent—and with magic. Compulsion. He was a vampire prince. Most likely turned by King Devin himself.

As if his compulsion would work on us. For as long as I could remember, the mages had given every supernatural on Avalon a black onyx ring that protected us from psychic attacks.

Thomas—also a vampire prince—stepped forward and looked the Tower vampire straight in the eyes. "My companions and I come from Avalon, under the order of the Earth Angel herself," he said. "We require an audience with King Devin at once."

The vampire prince snarled. "You teleport here—uninvited—and expect the king to be at your disposal?"

"Avalon is allied with the Tower in the war against the demons," Thomas reminded him. "We all answer to the Earth Angel."

"And all meetings are arranged by the Earth Angel and King Devin," he said. "But King Devin told us nothing about a meeting."

I stepped forward, unable to contain myself for a

second longer. "We were sent here by the granddaughter of the former head witch of the Tower," I said. "She passed along some very interesting—and very *private*—information about one of King Devin's affairs."

"Mind your place, woman," said the shifter next to the vampire prince. "Or should I say, girl? You lack the maturity of a *real* woman." He licked his lips, his leech-like gaze traveling over to Sage.

Sage's eyes hardened. "We're here to discuss the information we've learned with the king, and only with the king. We have every reason to believe this is personal information he wants kept secret. But if he won't grant us an audience..." She let the sentence hang, the implication enough to get her threat across.

The shifter growled. But the vampire guard stuck his hand in front of him, stopping him from attacking.

"What's the name of this former head witch of the Tower?" He directed his question to Thomas.

"We only have a first name," Thomas said. "Donatella."

The vampire prince's nostrils flared the moment Thomas uttered Donatella's name. "You'll be escorted to the lobby, where you'll have your identities confirmed," he said. The other guards looked at him in shock, but he continued, ignoring their surprised expressions. "I'll go to King Devin and see if he's willing to speak with you. But first—surrender your weapons."

Reed's hand went protectively to the handle of his sword. "You'll return them to us when we leave?" he asked.

"*If* you leave, then yes, we'll return your weapons."

"'If?'" Thomas stared down the vampire prince in challenge.

"Yes—if," he said. "If you are who you say you are. And if you're truly here by the orders of the Earth Angel. After all, like you said—we're allies. We can't have our allies deceiving us, can we?"

"We're not deceiving you," Reed all but growled.

"Good," he said. "Then follow the guards to the lobby. I'll meet you there once I've spoken with the king."

The sleek lobby was full of supernatural patrons at bustling bars and restaurants. Women in short, tight dresses clung onto the men they were with, remaining mostly silent as the men spoke amongst themselves.

Shifters took our blood samples and hurried away with them—assumedly to an apothecary where witches would examine them. Guards surrounded our table, standing stick straight and looking blankly ahead.

Thomas looked around intensely, presumably tuning in to the technology around us. His gift of controlling technology was a huge asset in a place like this. Given all the security cameras, he probably had a detailed map of the entire complex in his head already.

The only people allowed near us were scantily clad human women holding round trays who asked if we wanted drinks. Well, they asked Thomas and Reed if they wanted drinks. They didn't speak to Sage or me.

The guys said no.

The women looked at Sage and me with pity, and scurried off to their next customers.

The vampire prince returned less than fifteen minutes later. "Come with me," he said.

Thomas stood up. Sage and Reed did the same.

I looked over at them in alarm. Because "come with me" could mean anything. He could be escorting us to the dungeon, for all we knew.

Reed gave me a single nod, as if reassuring me it would be okay.

It will *be okay*, I told myself. *Throwing us into the dungeon would break the Tower's alliance with Avalon. Our kingdoms might not like each other much, but we share an enemy. We're on the same side. At least until the demons are defeated.*

I stood up, and we followed the guard into the center of the grouping of skyscrapers, where an elevator waited with its doors open for us to enter.

TORRENCE

The elevator had glass walls, so we could look out at the complex surrounding us. It took us straight up to the topmost floor of the central—and tallest—skyscraper in the kingdom.

The doors opened, and we stepped into the two-storied foyer of a grand apartment. Two sets of stairs curved around the entryway, the floors and the walls covered in shiny black marble.

The guard led us back to a sitting area with a giant floor-to-ceiling window overlooking the entire city.

King Devin sat on a couch facing us, dressed in black jeans and a matching leather jacket.

Three frail, human women in corsets and fishnet tights sat around him. One of them had her wrist raised to his mouth as he drank her blood straight from the vein. Her neck was tilted back in pleasure—she didn't even notice our arrival.

But King Devin did, because he pushed her wrist away from his mouth and dropped it into her lap.

She blinked a few times and looked to him in question.

"Go to my room," he commanded. "We'll finish this later."

The women stood, although the one wobbled from blood loss. The other two rushed toward her to help her balance. Hanging on to one another, they hurried down the hall and up the grand staircase.

Once they were gone, King Devin wiped the excess blood from his lips and stood up. "I rarely let anyone interrupt my feedings," he said, finally focusing on the group of us. "But Gustavo here tells me that you mentioned an old head witch of mine whose name I haven't heard for decades."

"Donatella," Thomas said.

"Dear, sweet Donatella." King Devin smiled, his grin laced with debauchery. "She was one of my favorites. Until she deserted me for that wretched kingdom full of unbridled females."

Unbridled. Like women were wild horses meant to be tamed.

I clenched my fists to my sides. But I held in my anger. Because I was there for Selena.

"Donatella's granddaughter told us you might have information we need," I said. "About how to get to the Otherworld."

King Devin's eyes flickered to me, and he frowned. "I'd like to learn why you're coming to me with this question," he said, looking back to Thomas. "But from you. You know how women are. They can't keep their stories straight and exaggerate until it's impossible to distinguish fact from fiction." He chuckled, although none of us joined in.

"I'm happy to tell you more." Thomas sounded more on edge than ever. "Perhaps we should sit down?"

King Devin tilted his head and looked around at the group of us. "The three of us men will sit," he said. "The women will remain standing, so we can admire their figures. And Gustavo—you're dismissed. Return to your post at once."

"Yes, sir." Gustavo saluted and left the apartment by elevator.

King Devin took a seat first, followed by Thomas and Reed. As instructed, Sage and I remained standing. It sucked, but we'd be out of there soon. For now, we had to do what we had to do.

Thomas quickly summarized everything that had happened up until now. "So, was Alice right?" he asked. "Do you know how we can get to the Otherworld?"

King Devin brought the pads of his fingers together into the shape of a tent. He studied Thomas, like he was debating how much he wanted to tell him.

"Please," I said, resting my hands on the back of the nearest armchair. "If you know something, tell us. We'll do anything to save Selena."

The king leaned back in the sofa and smirked. Then he looked over at Reed. "I love it when women beg," he said. "Especially the young ones. Don't you?"

Reed pressed his lips together. His eyes were hard, like it was taking some serious effort to keep himself from blowing up at King Devin then and there.

"You haven't said we're wrong," Reed finally said, each word calm and measured.

"I haven't. But you don't expect me to give you this information for free, do you?"

"We're allies," Thomas said. "So, yes. That's exactly what we expect you to do."

"We're allies in the war against the demons," King Devin said. "But the demons didn't take the Earth Angel's daughter. That was purely the fae."

Anger swirled in my blood like magma. "Allies are

supposed to help each other be the best they can be," I said. "Avalon is at its best when Selena is there."

"You know nothing about the politics between vampire kingdoms, child," King Devin snapped, and I recoiled at the harshness of his tone. "Stay out of this and let the men do the talking."

Thomas narrowed his eyes at me, and his message was clear. Be quiet and let him handle King Devin.

"Sorry," Thomas apologized on my behalf. "As you said, Torrence is young. She misspoke."

King Devin nodded in acceptance of Thomas's apology and leaned back in the sofa again. "It's such a bother that we need witches to teleport us from place to place," he said. "Especially if our strongest ones are also the feistiest. After enough transgressions, I find cutting out the tongue and refusing them the ingredients for healing potion to be an ideal solution. They can't talk back if they can't speak." He glanced back at me, like it was a threat.

Disgust rolled through me, and I had to swallow to keep myself from getting sick all over King Devin's polished marble floor.

Why had the Earth Angel agreed to an alliance with this *monster*?

Reed moved closer to the edge of his seat. "Attacking a citizen of Avalon is a declaration of war," he said.

"Did you see me attack anyone?" King Devin raised his hands in a ridiculous display of innocence. "I was simply trying to give you advice."

"Noted," Thomas said. "But as much as you dislike listening to her, Torrence made a good point. The Earth Angel needs to be at her best to make decisions regarding the war against the demons. She can't do that when her daughter and her husband are being held by the fae."

King Devin all but rolled his eyes. "What an interesting—yet pathetic—way of trying to twist the situation," he said.

Thomas opened his mouth to say more, but King Devin raised a hand, stopping him.

"The Tower doesn't owe you information about the Otherworld to hold true to our alliance," he said. "But I'll tell you what you want to know. For a price."

"Name it," Sage said.

"Aren't you an eager little thing?" King Devin chuckled again.

We all stared him down, waiting for him to be out with it.

"I see you're impatient to get down to business," he said. "But we've yet to break bread together. Have you no respect for tradition?"

Reed cracked his knuckles, like he was one step away

from punching King Devin in the jaw. "I've heard this area of the world is known for its steak," he said.

"We do have excellent steak." King Devin smiled. "Imported fresh from Argentina."

"Wonderful." Sage flashed her teeth. "I'm starving, and steak sounds delicious."

King Devin looked at her with pity. "How unfortunate," he said. "Because you've arrived right after dinner."

What was he planning on doing? Starving us?

"What a shame." I matched King Devin's knowing smile with one of my own. "I suppose dessert will do."

"I was enjoying my dessert before the four of you interrupted," he said. "I've been rather impatient to return to it. But I'd love to treat you to the finest steak the Tower has to offer. We'll enjoy it in my private dining room at the same time tomorrow."

"No." My eyes widened in horror. "If we wait until tomorrow, an entire *week* will have passed in the Otherworld."

"Do you want me to share this information with you or not?" he asked.

"Of course we do," Thomas cut in before I could say another word. "But perhaps it would be easiest to have a small bite sent up for us now. That way we can be out of your hair and you can return to business as usual." He glanced at where the three human women had disappeared down the hall.

"I just invited you to a dinner of the finest steak on the continent." Anger rose in King Devin's tone. "Do you truly have the gall to *refuse* me?"

"Not refuse." Thomas remained calm. "Your offer is extremely generous. But given the situation, a rain check would be appreciated."

King Devin stood up. Thomas and Reed immediately did the same. "The offer is for tomorrow night, and *only* for tomorrow night," he fumed. "No meal, no deal."

He stared Thomas down, daring him to contradict him.

I knew stubbornness when I saw it. The king wasn't going to budge.

A pit formed in my stomach at the thought of Selena having to spend another week in the Otherworld. But King Devin was the best chance we had of getting to her.

We needed him a lot more than he needed us.

Thomas looked to us, and I nodded to give him the okay. Reed and Sage did the same.

"All right," Thomas said. "We agree to your terms."

King Devin smiled, immediately placated. "Wonderful." He gave Thomas's hand a firm shake. "Return to the lobby. I'll call down to tell the staff to have rooms readied for you, and I'll see you back here tomorrow."

SELENA

I'D THOUGHT the Coliseum was huge... but that was before seeing the Circus Maximus.

The circus looked like someone had taken the Coliseum and stretched it out, so the inside was the shape of a long oval. The center of the arena was set up in two lanes, with ten giant marble statues at the end of each one. At the far ends of each lane were two bronze discs, each one the size of a large pizza.

Tons and tons of seats surrounded the center of the circus. There must have been five times as many seats as in the Coliseum. They were all full, although the fae and half-bloods were giddy and chatty as they enjoyed their drinks and snacks. It was a far cry from their raucous behavior during the fight to the death in the Coliseum.

Just like in the Coliseum, the other players and I were escorted to a special box reserved for the chosen champions. They all wore their fighting gear. Since I was the outgoing Empress of the Villa and couldn't participate in this competition, I wore another gown, along with the golden wreath on my head.

Sorcha didn't join us. Apparently, she only graced the empire with her presence during the fights to the death. I didn't spot Prince Devyn in the front rows with the other royal fae, either.

All eyes were on us as we entered, and I was numb as I sat on the throne. That was how I'd felt since watching Octavia and Emmet murder Molly yesterday. Numb.

Molly's final moments kept replaying in my mind. All I could do was watch it over and over, lost in a loop of theories about everything I could have done differently to prevent her death from happening.

There was a *lot* I could have done. I'd screwed up my week as Empress of the Villa big time.

Suddenly, Bacchus appeared in a flash of light, snapping me back into focus.

He flew his chariot in laps around the circus. With his bright purple toga and wide grin, he'd returned to his persona of "jovial Bacchus"—opposed to the "dark Bacchus" from the Coliseum.

The crowd cheered, but it was excited, happy cheering. Far different from the bloodthirsty cries of yesterday.

Finally, Bacchus landed his chariot on top of the wide divider line between the lanes. "Welcome to the second Emperor of the Villa competition!" he said, and the crowd erupted into applause. "That was an exciting battle in the arena yesterday, wasn't it?"

The audience cheered louder, hooting and hollering in appreciation of the fight.

I gripped my hands into fists so tightly that my nails dug into my palms.

After what felt like ages, Bacchus raised his scepter, quieting the crowd. "After two brutal competitions in a row, the other gods and I thought it was time for something more lighthearted," he said. "Discus throwing. As you can see, there are ten statues at the end of each lane. Statues of the false Norse gods."

The crowd gave a collective boo at the mention of the Norse gods.

Bacchus smiled, pleased with this reaction. "The chosen champions will face off in pairs, throwing their discuses at the statues," he said. "The first champion to knock down all ten statues will win that round. The loser of each round will be knocked out of the competition."

He paused to survey the crowd. Many had taken their seats again as they listened to the rules.

"There are invisible boundaries around each lane so the champions can't interfere with each other's progress," Bacchus said. "This is an *individual* competition—no attacking each other allowed. And using magic to knock down the statues is against the rules and will result in elimination from the competition. The statues *must* be knocked down with the discus." He looked to all of us sitting in the box, checking to make sure we understood.

We did.

"The outgoing Empress of the Villa—Selena, the chosen champion of Jupiter—will select the first two champions to face off," he continued. "The winner of that round will select who he or she wants to see face off next, and so on and so forth. This will continue until only one champion remains. That champion will be this week's Emperor of the Villa."

He paused, taking a few seconds to examine the crowd. They looked interested, but not *as* excited as they had for any of the competitions or demonstrations we'd had in the Games so far.

"But just because this competition is more light-hearted, it doesn't mean it has to be less entertaining!" Bacchus said, and the crowd instantly perked up.

"Because to add a little something special to the spectacle, I've added a personal trademark of mine into the sport."

He gave a flourish with his free hand, and a goblet of wine appeared in it. At the same time, two pedestals with large goblets of wine on them appeared on the far end of each lane, a few feet behind the discuses.

"Before each champion can pick up his or her discus and start aiming for the statues, they have to drink all of the liquid in their goblet," he said. "And trust me, this wine isn't the watered-down stuff. It's strong. You can bet they'll be feeling it—especially with each new round they play." He raised his goblet in a toast, and the crowd went wild. "So, who's ready to watch a drunken discus throwing competition?!"

Cheers erupted from the crowd once more. Many of them raised their wine glasses and chugged them down.

My chest tightened so I could barely breathe, my stomach swirling in disgust. They didn't care that by the end of the week, another one of us would be dead. This was just a spectacle to them.

They didn't see us as people. All they saw were pawns in a game designed for their entertainment.

I was trapped on their chessboard. The only way to escape was to win.

Bacchus pounded his scepter on the ground beside

his chariot, and everyone focused on him. "Selena, chosen champion of Jupiter," he said. "Select the two champions that you want to see face off first."

I gulped and looked at the others before me. Choosing who faced off first was a big deal. I refused to mess up like I had when selecting the players to send to the arena.

Octavia was a given.

As for the second champion... that was the challenging part of this decision. I didn't want to choose an ally, because I wanted my allies to have a good chance at getting far in the competition. That wouldn't happen if they played in too many rounds, because the more wine they drank, the sloppier they'd get.

At the same time, I didn't want to choose someone like Emmet, who'd just betrayed me. He'd made it clear in the arena that he'd picked a side, and it wasn't mine. He'd be more likely to send two of *my* allies to face off if he won the round. So he—and anyone else who might support Octavia—was a no go.

I needed someone neutral. Someone unpredictable. Someone who I thought could beat Octavia, but who wouldn't decide to come after me later for choosing them to face off first.

"Selena," Bacchus said. "You're taking too much time. Make your choice now."

"I choose Octavia, the chosen champion of Neptune," I said, and Octavia rolled her eyes, since she'd clearly expected it. "And Antonia, the chosen champion of Apollo."

25

SELENA

THE MOMENT after I said Antonia's name, Bridget nodded in approval. Good. I was pretty sure that out of all of us, Bridget knew and understood the Games the best.

I was definitely going to listen to her advice more from this point forward.

Octavia and Antonia took their places at the end of each lane, and I became more and more confident of my decision. Because as the chosen champion of Apollo, Antonia had nearly perfect aim. If anyone could knock down those statues before Octavia, it was her.

"Pick up your goblets of wine," Bacchus instructed, and the two of them did as he said. The goblets were nearly as big as their heads. "One, two, three… CHUG!"

Antonia raised the goblet to her lips and started chugging the wine.

Octavia created an orb of blue magic with her hands, just big enough to surround her goblet. The magic sparkled and swirled, the light reflecting off her smirking face.

"She's not allowed to do that," I said, although my voice was drowned out amongst the cheering crowd. No one looked at me, and I quickly thought back to the rules Bacchus had announced earlier.

Champions weren't allowed to use magic to *knock down the statues*. But using magic on the wine was fair game.

Octavia's blue orb of magic disappeared from around the goblet. Smiling, she raised it to her lips and started to drink.

Antonia finished drinking first. She put the goblet back down and rubbed at her temples, her eyes dizzy. Then she stumbled toward the discus, unable to walk in a straight line.

Crap. Antonia was a small girl... and she was also apparently a lightweight. I'd had to make my decision so quickly that I'd forgotten to take that into account.

She picked up the discus and hurled it toward the statues. I wasn't sure which statue she was aiming for, but it chipped off one on the right, grazing its shoulder but not knocking it down.

She ran to retrieve the discus and ran back to the starting point of the lane, wiping a bead of sweat from her brow.

Her second throw didn't go any better than the first.

By the time Antonia was on her third throw, Octavia finished her wine and strutted over to pick up her discus. She walked completely straight. If she felt anything from the wine, she was doing an impressive job of hiding it.

She picked up the discus, hurled it toward the statues... and missed.

I let out a breath of relief. Especially because a second later, Antonia knocked down her first statue.

Unfortunately, Octavia's next throw hit the center statue in the stomach. A loud BOOM echoed through the arena as the statue exploded into pieces and fell to the ground.

It continued on like that for minutes, with them both missing and destroying the statues at random. But as they continued, Antonia got more and more sluggish. Her face was flushed bright pink. She was still hitting a few of the statues, but she was slowing down considerably.

Before I knew it, Octavia had two statues left, and

then only one.

She picked up her discus, held it in the air in an early victory celebration, and hurled it toward the statue.

It hit the statue straight in the center.

The stone exploded and crumbled to pieces.

The moment it was destroyed, Antonia dropped her discus and sat on the ground, holding her head between her hands and rubbing her temples.

My stomach sunk to my feet.

"Octavia has won this round!" Bacchus announced, his eyes wild as he pointed his scepter toward the statues. They pieced back together and righted themselves, so they were exactly how they'd been at the start of the competition. "Antonia will return to the Champions' Box and stand at the back, to signify that she's out of the competition. But first—Octavia, select the two champions who will be facing off next."

"Easy." Octavia smirked and tossed her hair over her shoulders, looking at me like she'd already won the entire thing. "I choose Cassia, the chosen champion of Ceres, and Julian, the chosen champion of Mars."

With his extreme strength, Julian quickly knocked Cassia out of the competition. He made it look like a piece of cake. Cassia barely had a chance to try.

Julian didn't hesitate before pitting Octavia and Emmet against each other.

The two of them marched confidently to their lanes. They even had the gall to high five each other before taking their places.

Bacchus counted off again. Emmet started chugging his wine, and Octavia surrounded her goblet with magic like she had before.

What was she doing to her goblet?

Emmet finished his wine and started throwing first. His aim was all right, although not as perfect as it would have been if he were allowed to use his power over air. He only managed to knock down one statue before Octavia finished her wine and walked over to her discus.

She walked as straight as before, *still* unaffected by the wine even though it was the second goblet she'd chugged. "Let me have this," she said to Emmet after he took a shot and missed another statue. "I'm using my magic to evaporate the alcohol out of the wine. This competition is mine."

Rage rushed through my veins, electricity surging through my body. Octavia was cheating.

But it wasn't technically cheating. Bacchus had specified that they had to drink all the *liquid* in their goblets.

By evaporating the alcohol out of the wine, it was no longer liquid.

The competition was rigged in Octavia's favor.

The lightning crackled more intensely under my skin. But I breathed slower, doing my best to meditate and channel Sorcha's calm demeanor. Acting out would only hurt me and my alliance-mates. I needed to keep my magic under control.

Julian's still in the competition, I reminded myself. *He's strong. He can beat Octavia. And I still have Bridget on my side, too.*

Emmet flung his discus forward, knocking down another statue. "Thanks for the offer," he said to Octavia. "But I'm here to compete."

Octavia snarled and destroyed another statue.

The round didn't take long, and it was close. But Octavia knocked down her statues first.

"Next up, I choose Julian, the chosen champion of Mars," she said. "To face off against Cillian, the chosen champion of Pluto."

I froze at Cillian's name. Apparently Octavia didn't care about pissing off Pluto's volatile champion. Which meant she *really* wanted to knock Julian out of the competition.

Come on Julian, I thought as he and Cillian stepped up to the lanes. *You've got this.*

They downed their goblets of wine, finishing around the same time. Then they walked up to grab their discuses, and luckily, Julian was still steady on his feet.

I held my breath as they took their first throws.

Julian destroyed one of his statues on the first try.

Cillian missed. By a *lot*. His discus would have flown into the audience if it weren't for the protective boundary around the lanes.

They went to retrieve their discuses, and Julian ran, like all the other champions had done. Cillian jogged at a steady pace.

I sat there, shocked as I watched Cillian's casual attitude.

He didn't want to be Emperor of the Villa.

There were a bunch of possible reasons why. But I didn't care. All that mattered was the relief I felt when Julian destroyed his final statue, and Cillian strolled back to the box to stand with the others who were out of the competition.

Next, Julian chose Octavia and Pierce to face off.

"I see how this is gonna be." Octavia glared at Julian as she and Pierce hurried to their places.

Why was Julian picking on Octavia? Octavia had it out for *me*—not for him. By making a show of trying to knock her out of the competition, he was drawing a line in the sand and painting a target on his back.

He's doing it to protect me.

My heart sped up, but I quickly shook away the thought. There were tons of other reasons to explain why Julian had it out for Octavia. And even if he *was* trying to protect me, it wasn't because he cared about me. It was because he thought I was an asset to our alliance.

By protecting me, he was protecting himself. That was all.

Octavia and Pierce picked up their goblets. But after Bacchus counted off, neither of them drank. Instead, they *both* used their magic. Pierce's orange magic surrounded his goblet just like Octavia's blue magic surrounded hers.

Fire. Pierce's magic was control over fire.

Fire evaporated alcohol.

I smiled at Julian, although he couldn't see, because his back was toward me as he watched the competition. Pitting Pierce against Octavia was smart.

Because Pierce and Octavia would both be sober as they faced off against each other.

I leaned forward, my entire body tense as I watched them throw their discuses and destroy their statues. They were both killing it. Octavia had the swing of it after so many previous rounds, and Pierce was just a force to be reckoned with.

Finally, they were down to one statue each.

The entire crowd was on their toes, watching with anticipation.

They flung their discuses, and the statues exploded in tandem, silencing the crowd.

"Wow!" Bacchus pointed his scepter toward the orbs floating throughout the circus, bringing them together to make a giant globe above his head. "It looks like we'll be taking a closer look to determine our winner!"

A holographic image flickered to life inside of the globe—a flashback to Pierce and Octavia right before taking their final shots.

Like before, their discuses flew toward the statues. But right before they hit, the recording slowed down so the discuses were moving so sluggishly that they might as well have been floating in place.

The discuses crept toward the statues, and I held my breath along with the rest of the crowd.

One of them hit its statue half a second before the other.

"Octavia!" Bacchus shouted her name above the cheers of the crowd. My stomach knotted, every bone in my body hollow as she raised her arms in victory. "You've won this round and will select the next two champions to face off in the competition!"

26

SELENA

OCTAVIA PITTED Julian and Bridget against each other.

Julian won, but he didn't have a choice to make, since Octavia and Felix were the only other remaining champions in the competition. Against Felix, Octavia won by a landslide.

With everyone else knocked out, Julian and Octavia were the only two champions left standing.

Well, Julian was *sort* of standing. By that point, he'd downed three giant goblets of Bacchus's insanely strong wine. He swayed as he walked in a wobbly line to the end of his lane, his eyes dizzy and unfocused. Once he reached the pedestal, he rested a hand on the edge of it to balance himself.

Come on, Julian, I thought. *Just one more round. You can do this.*

He *had* to do it. My life in the Games depended on it.

Bacchus counted down, and Julian and Octavia reached for their goblets.

As always, Octavia used her magic to evaporate the alcohol out of the wine.

Julian stared down the center of his, swallowing like he was about to be sick. But he raised the goblet to his lips anyway, forcing down the liquid much slower than he had before.

From the disgusted way Octavia looked down into her goblet after evaporating the alcohol, it was obvious that the sheer amount of liquid they were consuming was a problem as well. But she also forced her drink down, finishing around the same time as Julian.

Julian held his head in his hands and took a few deep breaths, trying to get ahold of himself. As he did, Octavia picked her discus off the ground and hurled it toward the statues.

BOOM. Her first statue exploded into pieces, and the crowd cheered in excitement.

They *wanted* Octavia to win. She was a monster, yet they were rooting for her.

Electricity rushed through me, and before I could process what was happening, my lightning exploded out of my hands.

It crashed into an invisible wall around the box and sizzled out.

People in the crowd looked my way and laughed. So I shot out another bolt, and another, and another. Each bolt released a bit of the anger building inside of me, but it didn't matter. Trapped in that glass box, I was all but powerless.

After a few more tries, I gasped and clenched my fists, gazing around at the crowd. Barely any of them looked my way anymore. They were all focused on Julian and Octavia.

Then I spotted two familiar faces diagonally across the way, far back in the lower tier. Finn and Bryan. The fae who had trained me in the days before the Games.

They were staring at me, their eyes hard in warning.

The sight of them anchored me in place. I needed to think back to my training. What would they tell me to do?

They'd tell me to control myself. They'd remind me that I wasn't helping Julian with this outburst. All I was doing was putting more of a target on my back—and the backs of the others in my alliance.

Even if Octavia becomes Empress of the Villa, it doesn't mean the end for me, I told myself. *If she sends me to the arena, I won't just lie down and die. I'll fight, and I'll live. I'll make sure of it.*

I sat straighter, returning my focus to Octavia and Julian. Octavia had four statues down, and Julian had two.

It wasn't ideal. But despite Octavia's advantage, the competition wouldn't be over until one of them had the golden wreath on their head.

Julian could still win.

He swayed even more after finishing that goblet. He was covered in sweat, and his aim was shot. So he was relying on brute strength to get through.

He threw the discus as hard and fast as he could, ran to get it, and repeated the process over and over. He barely paused, minus a few stumbles running to get the discus and coming back with it.

He was managing to destroy a decent number of statues that way.

But Octavia didn't miss. She destroyed one statue after another, until eventually, they were all down.

Julian collapsed onto his knees and rested his forehead on the dirt. He pounded his fists into the ground, and the entire arena shook with the force of his strength.

Defeat crashed upon me. I couldn't move. I was frozen on the throne, watching Octavia pull her dark hair out of its ponytail and shake it out to blow freely over her shoulders as the crowd cheered her name.

This can't be happening.

Bacchus flew his chariot to the ground in front of her and raised his goblet of wine in a toast. "Congratulations to our new Empress of the Villa—Octavia, the chosen champion of Neptune!" he said, and the crowd cheered and toasted with him. "Step up to the throne in the Champions Box, where the previous Empress of the Villa will crown you with the golden wreath."

Octavia smirked the entire time she walked toward me. But I held her gaze, not wanting to look weak by glancing away.

She might have power for the next week. But I refused to let her break me. I'd get through this, somehow. I had to.

Her face was covered in sweat, dirt sticking to it like war paint. She kneeled before me, her dangerous, ocean blue gaze never leaving mine.

My palms hummed with electricity. It would be so easy to reach forward and jolt her at high force, killing her on the spot. My magic danced faster with the thought of it, my hands and arms glowing with the lightning running through them.

"You want to kill me." She smiled sweetly, her voice full of venom. "Do it. I dare you. Do it, and we'll both die."

Disgust rose up my throat—because she was right.

I'd never thought of myself as capable of murder. But a few seconds ago, I'd truly wanted to kill her with every bit of magic in my body.

I glanced away from her, my chest hollow as I observed the cheering, bloodthirsty crowd around us.

I won't let them win.

I might have been thrust into these Games against my will. But I refused to let them turn me into a monster. Even if I was forced to kill or be killed, I'd do it with a heavy heart, and take no joy from it.

The electricity rushing through me dulled to a low throb until the glowing bolts disappeared from my skin.

"You may be my enemy in the Games," I said, reaching up to remove the wreath from my head. "But that doesn't mean you deserve to die."

Even as I placed the wreath gently on Octavia's head, she looked as angry as ever.

"I don't care how 'special' everyone thinks you are." She narrowed her eyes, like everything about me disgusted her. "Sure, you may have powerful magic. But your heart is soft. And that's going to get you killed."

I didn't have time to reply before she spun around, her back toward me as she raised her arms above her head and soaked in the crowd's applause.

Dread curled through me. Octavia was officially Empress of the Villa.

And by the end of the week, I expected to be in the ring at the Coliseum, fighting for my life.

27

SELENA

THE BANQUET that night in honor of Octavia's Empress of the Villa win was torturous.

Julian and I sat across from each other, neither of us speaking to one another. Felix sat next to Octavia, making sure her wine glass remained full. Pierce and Emmet sat close to her as well, joking and bantering like brothers.

Even Bridget and Cassia pretended to make nice with Octavia. I didn't blame them—of course they wanted to avoid being sent to the arena. But it didn't change the fact that every time one of them chatted with her, it felt like a knife of betrayal stabbing me in the back, over and over and over again.

The only one who was as quiet as me and Julian was

Cillian. He just sat there, stabbing his food and glaring at everyone with his creepy eyes that were as dark as night.

Once dinner was over, Octavia breezed by me on the way up to her suite. "Don't even bother trying to come up to talk with me," she said. "I won't let you in. And it's best you save your breath, since nothing you can say or do will change my mind."

I believed her.

And she was right that I should save my energy. Because I had more important things to do.

I needed to learn how to master my magic so I'd have a fighting chance in that arena.

That night, I lay in the giant room I shared with the other girls in the villa, waiting for them to go to sleep. Once positive they were out cold, I sneaked out, tiptoed over to the guys' room, and pressed my ear against their door. All was quiet in there, too. The light was off upstairs in Octavia's suite as well.

They were all exhausted—or hungover—after the competition today. Which was perfect for me.

Because with everyone sound asleep, I stepped into the back yard of the villa. It was fenced in—a fence went around the entire house—but it was the largest area of open space we had. The aurora danced beautifully in the sky, a stunning mix of greens, pinks, and purples.

I walked to the end of the yard near the fence, not wanting to risk waking anyone up.

If only I had witch powers. Then I could cast a sound barrier spell and make sure no one hears me.

But I didn't have witch powers. So I was just going to do the best with what I had. Besides, what would the others do if they knew I was practicing my magic to use it against them? Kill me?

They already wanted to do that.

So I truly had nothing to lose.

The back yard was full of trees with branches that wept like umbrellas. Occasional sticks and twigs were scattered across the grass.

I could work with this.

I gathered some of the sticks, placed them in a row on the ground, kneeled down to get closer to them, and rubbed my hands together.

Okay, lightning. Time to do your thing.

I gathered up the sparks of electricity humming through my body until my hands and arms glowed with power. In training, this was when I'd touch an object and make it combust.

But I'd proven multiple times in the Games that I was capable of doing so much more than that.

All I needed was to learn how to control it.

I held my arm out straight in front of me, picturing a

bolt of lightning shooting out of my palm and striking the nearest branch.

The light in my hand flickered and dimmed out.

Seriously?

I glared at the branch and shook my hands out a few times, like they were broken objects I could repair by fiddling with them a bit.

Nothing happened.

I tried gathering my electricity a few more times, waiting until it buzzed brighter and stronger before shooting it toward the branches.

But as hard as I tried to push the lightning out of my palms, it just wouldn't *go*.

Don't get defeated, I told myself, standing up and stretching my hands behind my back. *It was only your first few tries. You didn't think you'd get this on your first few tries, did you?*

After how easily the bolts had come to me those other times, yeah, I kind of did. But then, I'd been fueled with emotion—rage and desperation.

That was what was missing now. Emotion. I'd been so focused on the actual, physical magic that I hadn't been thinking about anything going on inside of me.

If I was being honest with myself, there was a reason for that. Because if I gave in to the pain and anger, I was afraid it would consume me until I didn't recognize myself anymore. Until I turned into the ruthless killer I feared I would become.

That couldn't happen.

But I felt like a ticking time bomb, just waiting to explode. That terrified me. Would I end up getting myself eliminated from the Games because my magic had more control over me than I had over it?

I refused to let that happen.

Which meant tapping into my feelings, but not giving in to them. If I did that, then I *should* be able to control the bolts.

I kneeled back down and took a deep breath. I could do this.

But before I could call on the electricity again, a twig snapped behind me.

I stood and spun around. My eyes instantly connected with Julian's ice blue ones.

"What are you doing here?" I asked, hiding my hands behind my back. "Shouldn't you be sleeping?"

"Shouldn't you?" He raised an eyebrow in challenge.

"Why are you so frustrating?" I stomped my foot into the ground.

He tilted his head, studying me. "Did you just stomp your foot?"

"Ugh." I groaned, glancing up at the aurora lighting

up the night sky before turning my attention back to him. "Stop answering my questions with questions."

"Why?" The corner of his lips lifted into a smirk.

"You're annoying," I said. "And I'm going inside."

"Wait." He reached out, his hand wrapping around my arm to stop me.

I froze and stared at him at the same moment as he realized what he'd done and pulled his hand back to his side.

"Sorry," he muttered, glancing down at the ground. "I shouldn't have done that."

I just stood there, stunned. Was the illusive chosen champion of Mars *embarrassed?*

No way. It was just an act. He was good at acting.

He'd proven that to me when he'd tricked me into trusting him so he could pull me through that portal.

At the reminder, I clenched my fists to my sides, glaring at him like he was the spawn of Satan.

If only he wasn't staring back with those captivating, intense eyes that looked so vulnerable. Damn Julian and his eyes. If he wasn't looking at me like that, maybe I could have hated him like I should have.

Instead, I hated myself for *not* hating him.

Talk about confusing.

"I came out here to practice," he said all at once.

I stepped back, jarred by his sudden admission. "Practice what?"

"Sword fighting," he said simply, like I should have figured it out on my own.

"But you're the chosen champion of Mars," I said. "You're a natural at sword fighting. You don't need to practice."

"Everyone needs to practice." He smiled, and his stupid smile was just as hypnotizing as his eyes. "Even the chosen champion of Mars. And apparently, the chosen champion of Jupiter, too." He nodded at where I was standing, like he'd just called me out.

"I'm not practicing," I lied. "I just came out here to... get some air."

From the amused way he looked at me, I could tell I was as terrible of a liar as I suspected.

And I just stood there like a mute idiot, unable to think of anything to say to make the lie more convincing. I cringed inwardly at how painfully awkward this entire encounter had been.

"Great timing, then." He broke the silence between us, and I felt like I could breathe again. "Because it's always better to practice with a sparring partner. You game?" He pulled two gleaming swords from the ether and held one out for me to take.

I kept my arms firmly to my sides, my eyes locked on

the sword. Part of me wanted to take it and get my anger out with the satisfying clash of the blade.

Another part of me worried that I'd continue fawning over Julian and make more of an idiot of myself than I already had. Being around him made it hard to think—and to speak. It was way too easy to get lost in his magnetic aura.

I'd already fallen once.

I didn't plan on being that naive girl that fell for him again.

"You *do* know how to sword fight," he said. "Right?"

"Of course I do." I kept my gaze level with his. "I grew up on a magical island, and I had no magic. Learning how to use a sword was the only thing I could do to have some way of defending myself."

"Well, this is working out perfectly." He held the sword higher, clearly expecting me to take it. "Let's do this."

But as I looked at the blade, suspicion rose in my chest. "Why do you want to practice with me?" I asked. "You know Octavia is probably sending us both to the arena. Right?"

His motive popped into my mind a second after the question left my mouth. He wasn't trying to *help* me.

He was trying to discover my weaknesses.

I was such an idiot for standing there talking to him

for so long. Sure, Julian and I had been in an alliance last week. But now that Octavia was Empress of the Villa, everything had changed.

I couldn't trust anyone. Especially not Julian, given the amount of frustrating, annoying power he had over my stupid emotions. Not only had I kissed him back on Earth, but I *still* turned into a bumbling idiot around him. Clearly, he realized his effect on me.

He had to be using me to ensure his survival in the Games.

"Octavia's probably sending us both to the arena," he agreed. "Which means we need to learn how to work together so we can take out whoever's in there with us."

My heart jumped into my throat.

I *wanted* to believe that he was offering to practice with me so we could both stay alive.

But he'd reeled me in like this before, only to turn on me quickly afterward. There was no reason why he wouldn't do the same thing again. No—he definitely *would* do the same thing again. He was ruthless. A true chosen champion of the god of war.

The only person I could trust in the Games was myself. I couldn't forget that.

I stepped back from the sword, my decision made. "No way am I showing you my cards," I said. "I'm tired, and I'm heading back inside. Have fun practicing with yourself."

"Oh, I will." He flashed me a knowing smile that hinted of something dangerous. Like he was positive that this wasn't over.

I shook away the butterflies fluttering in my stomach as I hurried back to the villa, forcing myself not to turn back to look at him.

Because if I did, I wasn't sure I'd have the strength to turn him down again.

28

SELENA

TODAY WAS THE DAY.

Octavia's Selection Ceremony.

We gathered in the library, the hearth burning brightly in front of the semi-circle of sofas and armchairs. I sat on a sofa between Cassia and Bridget. Cassia was as fidgety as ever. Bridget was as still as a statue.

Earlier that morning, I'd asked Bridget if she'd had any visions telling her who Octavia would select for the arena. She'd said no. But from the stiff way she was sitting—like she was ready for what was coming—I couldn't help but suspect she'd lied.

Julian was in the armchair across from me. He didn't look my way. Instead, he was chatting with Antonia and Felix, of all people.

Doesn't Julian hate Felix?

Finally, the doors opened. We all silenced and turned around, watching Octavia and Vesta walk inside.

Octavia looked like a queen in a gorgeous ocean-blue gown. She wore loads of gold jewelry, similar to what I'd worn last week. Her straight dark hair hung perfectly down her back, and the golden wreath sat on her head.

The orbs floated behind her, recording every move.

She and Vesta reached the front of the room, and Vesta introduced her to the viewers. It was all for show, of course, since the viewers already knew who we were. But it was the tradition of the ceremony.

"Octavia," Vesta continued. "Please take my place in front of the hearth and make your selections."

With her chin held high, Octavia stepped to the front of the room and faced us. Three of the orbs followed her, settling down to hover in front of her waist.

"I'll touch each orb and toss it into the air," she said the line that all Emperors of the Villa were required to say during the ceremony. "The face of the selected champion will appear in the orb, locking in each decision of who I'll be sending to the arena."

My chest tightened, and time felt like it was standing still. Unless a strange miracle happened and Octavia suddenly decided I wasn't enemy number one, I expected to see my face in one of those orbs.

Octavia reached forward, grabbed the first orb, and tossed it into the air.

It floated above her head, my face appearing as a hologram in the center.

My head buzzed, and every background noise in the room became muffled. I couldn't move. I could barely think.

All I could do was stare in horror at my face in the orb looking back at me.

"Selena, chosen champion of Jupiter," Octavia said, her eyes full of glee as she looked at me. "I've selected you because as the first ever chosen champion of Jupiter, you're a wild card with your magic. I don't like that. I also don't like you."

Electricity buzzed through me, bringing me out of my shocked trance. "The feeling's mutual," I replied, somehow sounding much more in control than I felt.

She smirked, reached for the next orb, and tossed it in the air.

Julian.

I glanced over at him, but he stared straight at the orb. His entire body was tight. He moved his focus to Octavia, holding her gaze with a lethal, challenging glare of his own.

"Julian, chosen champion of Mars," Octavia said. "You made it clear in the Emperor of the Villa competition that you're coming after me. It would be stupid of me not to send you to the arena this week."

He nodded, like he'd expected nothing less.

She looked away from him and grabbed the final orb. But instead of throwing it immediately into the air, she held onto it and stared at it.

Was she still undecided about the third person she was sending to the arena?

Please don't choose Cassia or Bridget, I thought, clenching my fists in my lap. *Or Cillian.*

Obviously I didn't want to fight against either of the two other people in my alliance. As for Cillian... he was more of a wild card than me, as far as I was concerned. With his strength *and* magic, he could be more dangerous than Julian and me combined.

After a few tense seconds, Octavia tossed the final orb into the air.

It settled next to the others above her head, and I gasped at the face staring out at us.

"Bridget, chosen champion of Minerva," Octavia said, and Bridget didn't move next to me. I glanced over my shoulder at her, but her gray eyes were blank. "You're the only champion who didn't come up to my suite to try making a deal with me. Minus Selena, of course, since I told her not to bother." She smirked at me again, and returned her focus to Bridget. "You're not my target. But if you don't want to work with me, I assume you're against me. Maybe that can be mended as the Games continue, or maybe not. But I hope you're able to use your gift of prophecy to figure out how to beat either Selena or Julian in the arena this week."

Bridget said nothing in return. Julian and I stayed silent, too.

Why didn't Bridget talk to Octavia after Octavia became Empress of the Villa? She could have tried making a deal with her. Something to ensure that Julian and I wouldn't have to face off against anyone in our alliance.

Before I could think of a possible answer, Vesta stepped up to stand beside Octavia. Her dress was the same color as the flames dancing behind her, and she held her hands delicately in front of herself, the ends of her sleeves draping down like an angel's robe. "Does anyone have anything to say?" She looked us over, focusing specifically on the three of us selected by Octavia.

"This is gonna be one hell of a match," Emmet jumped in, grinning when the orbs buzzed faster around him.

"Yeah it will be!" Pierce gave Emmet a high five. "It's about time we saw the full force of Selena's magic in action."

Everyone except for Julian, Bridget, and Cassia nodded and murmured in agreement.

I stared down at my hands, every part of me numb. If my practice session last night was any indication, they were in for a major disappointment.

Especially because I couldn't see myself turning on Bridget or Julian. Revulsion twisted in my stomach at either option.

Even after what Julian had done to me, the thought of hurting him made me feel sick. He couldn't die. He just *couldn't*. The mere possibility of a world without him in it made me feel empty all the way to the center of my bones.

How am I supposed to do this?

"Thank you, Octavia." Vesta's warm voice broke through my fear, bringing everything back into focus again. "This Selection Ceremony has come to a close. The selected champions will remain in the villa until we all go to the arena." She looked away from the orbs and focused on me, Julian, and Bridget. "I wish the three of you the best of luck."

SELENA

THAT NIGHT, I waited till everyone was asleep again. Then, I went to the back yard for another practice session.

The only things around me were the annoying golden orbs. Other than them, it looked like this time, I'd be free to practice in private.

My sticks were all lined up in the row I'd placed them in last night. Interesting. No one else ventured this far back in the yard, but Julian *had* to have seen them. Why had he left them untouched?

I didn't know, and I tried not to care. Because I had some serious practicing to do.

I tried, and tried, and tried to call on bolts and shoot them toward the sticks. I *felt* the magic inside of me. But it wasn't going any better tonight than it had last night. I even stared at the orbs to try calling upon the anger I'd felt during the Magic Demonstration Ceremony. It didn't work.

Probably because there wasn't a crowd around me screaming about how much of a disappointment I was. And as much as I tried imagining that the crowd was around me saying those same things, it wasn't the same as actually *being* there.

After thirty minutes of trying and failing, I picked up one of the sticks and threw it onto the ground. This was hopeless.

"Having trouble harnessing your magic?" a familiar voice said from behind me.

Julian.

I spun around and saw him leaning against a tree.

How long had he been watching me?

Apparently, long enough to realize what I was doing.

"How do you keep sneaking up on me like this?" I asked. "I should have heard you."

"You were focused," he said. "And being so quiet that I can launch silent attacks is part of my war gift."

"Oh," I said. "That's… convenient."

It was also another thing I needed to be aware of when we faced off in the arena.

"It is," he said. "But now you're the one avoiding my questions. You can't harness your magic, can you?"

He was right, and we both knew it. But why did he have to be so *smug* about it?

"What's it to you?" I asked.

"I know you don't believe me," he said. "But I don't want you to die in the arena at the end of the week."

"You're right. I don't believe you." I wanted to mean it, but a part of me *wanted* him to be telling the truth.

That part of me needed a serious reality check.

"That's fair." He stood straight and walked toward me. With each step closer, my breath grew more and more shallow. He stopped when there were only a few feet left between us, and then, I could breathe again. "Would you believe me if I said I wanted to help you learn how to create your bolts at will?"

I studied him, unsure what his motives were. He *had* to be toying with me.

Maybe he didn't believe I could do it, and he wanted to tear at my confidence before we entered the arena. Maybe he was trying to learn my strengths and weaknesses so he'd know how to best launch an attack.

As I contemplated his offer, he held my gaze, like he was daring me to say no.

"I want to help you." He held his hands up in a peace offering. "I swear it."

He was too skilled at lying for his own good.

"Why would you help me when we're pitted against

each other?" I clenched my fists, my magic crackling and sparking under my skin. "I'm nothing to you. I'm just another champion in your way. And I have the best reason out of all of us to *hate* you, since I'm only here because you tricked me, stole me away, and sold me out. You should be protecting yourself against me. Not offering to help me."

My magic burned bright, my hands and arms glowing with spider webs of electricity surging through my veins.

Harness it.

I opened my palms downward and pushed my magic through them with everything I had.

Two tiny bolts shot out of my hands and struck the ground.

They flashed out after a split second, leaving tiny scorched craters in their wake. Thin tendrils of smoke rose up from where they'd struck.

I froze, shocked that I'd actually done it. Then I relaxed and took a deep breath, relishing in the smoky smell of victory.

"Look at that." Julian beamed at the craters. "I'm already helping."

"Only because your mere existence pisses me off."

He smirked, like I'd proven his point. "Then I'm the perfect person to help you master your magic," he said.

I stared at him, waiting for a catch. There *had* to be a catch.

"You're doing this because you want to make some kind of deal in the Games with me, aren't you?" I asked.

"I'm not here to make a deal." He looked at the ground and shuffled his feet, like he was nervous. Then he raised his gaze to meet mine again. "But I'm hoping you'll accept my help as an apology for what I did."

"Seriously?" I balked. "You kidnapped me and traded me for *money*. I'll never, ever forget or forgive you for that."

"You're right." He ran his hand through his hair and glanced up at the waxing moon, like he was looking to it for guidance. "I wish I'd gotten those coins a different way. But do you remember what I told you back at the fountain? About my sister being sick?"

"I do."

"It was true," he said. "My sister and I were young when our father was chosen for the Games. He died in them."

"I'm sorry," I said, since no matter how awful of a person Julian might be, no one deserved to suffer the loss of a parent when they were so young.

He nodded and pressed his lips together, obviously not wanting to think about his father. "Right afterward, Vita—my sister—got sick," he continued. "A chronic stomach thing, just like I told you at the fountain. There's no cure, but there are herbs that make the pain manageable. *Expensive* herbs. For a while, our friends and neighbors helped out, contributing what they could to make sure she got her medicine. But once they realized she wasn't going to be cured, they stopped. We've been barely scraping by these past few years to afford them. Even then, we don't have enough. She *needs* those herbs. Without them..." He shook his head and swallowed, unable to continue.

"So you decided to what—go into the business of trading people for money?" I stepped back, keeping my gaze locked on his. "You became some kind of hit man?"

"Sort of," he said, completely unapologetic about it. "But I only hunt the people who deserve it."

"So now you're some kind of angel of death." This wasn't making him sound any better. In fact, he was only sounding more and more like a monster.

"I don't kill anyone," he said sharply—so sharply that I believed he was telling the truth. "But I do scare them. Make them realize that whatever they've been doing to make someone send me after them needs to stop, before someone far less merciful than me comes their way."

"Fine," I said. "But you said you only come after people who deserve it. I didn't deserve it."

"You're right," he said. "But the amount of gold coins

that Prince Devyn offered me…" He trailed off and rubbed the back of his neck, like he was trying to think of the right way to phrase it. "I couldn't turn it down. You see, in the past few months, rumors about a Wild Plague have been spreading throughout the Otherworld. It supposedly originated deep in the Western Wildlands. But if it exists, it hasn't hit here yet. No one here has even *seen* anyone with the plague—at least not anyone I know and trust."

I shifted my weight from one leg to the other, uncomfortable with how open he was suddenly being. "What does this plague have to do with me?" I asked.

"It has to do with Vita," he said. "Our neighbors are starting to talk. They think she might have the Wild Plague."

"But that's impossible," I said. "She got sick before the plague even existed!"

"That's *if* the plague exists at all," he said. "And yes, it's ridiculous. But people love to gossip, and rumors of the Wild Plague terrify them. They want to keep the plague far, far away. With the way they've been talking, I worry it won't be long before they kick Vita out of the citadel—or worse."

His eyes darkened, and I shivered.

I didn't want to think his own people would murder his sister for having a chronic stomach illness. But these were the same people who were watching us fight to the death for entertainment. They were capable of anything.

"If I win the Faerie Games, Vita and my mother will be protected by the Empress herself," he continued. "They'll be given enough coin to live in comfort for the rest of their lives. Vita will have her medicine, and she'll be able to live a normal life. She'll grow up, fall in love, and eventually start a family of her own. I'm the only one who can give that to her. So that's exactly what I plan on doing."

He stood strong and determined—like winning the Games was his destiny.

"I understand why you entered the Faerie Games," I said, since I did. "And as much as I hate to admit it, I can kind of understand why you took Prince Devyn up on his offer. You needed to make sure your sister and mother were taken care of while you're away."

"Exactly." His lips curved up into a small, hopeful smile.

"But by bringing me here, you all but sentenced me to death." Heated rage burned through me, and his smile vanished. If he thought his sob story would make me forgive him for *ruining my life*, he had another thing coming.

"I know." He reached forward, but pulled his arm back at the last second. "I've regretted it since we portaled into Prince Devyn's courtyard and I saw you in your true form."

"Seriously?" My mouth dropped open in disbelief, and I quickly closed it. "You're saying that if I truly looked like Torrence, you wouldn't have regretted what you'd done? You regret it because what... you think I'm pretty?"

It sounded absurd, but I couldn't think of what else he might have meant.

He scowled. "You make it sound like such an awful thing."

"Because it *is* awful."

The orbs buzzed faster. I'd been getting used to their presence—but the entire time we'd been talking about the Wild Plague, they'd dimmed and had stopped circling us.

Apparently, whoever decided what the live viewers were going to see didn't want them hearing about the Wild Plague.

"Maybe it is," he said, and I looked away from the orbs, taken aback by the fiery passion in his ice blue eyes. "But it's the truth. Something about you..." He paused to gather his thoughts, studying me like I was an enigma.

I was breathless as I waited for him to continue.

Does he feel the same pull to me that I feel to him? The

conversation I'd had with Felix last week rushed through my mind. *Could Julian and I be soulmates?*

No. That was impossible.

What kind of cruel trick would the Universe be pulling on us by making us soulmates and then throwing us into a game to the death?

"I can't explain it." He threw his hands out in frustration. "But I know that no matter what, I wouldn't be able to kill you. Which gives me only one option. I have to work *with* you."

"You make it sound so awful," I said.

"It is." Darkness crossed over his face, and for the first time that night, he looked at me like *I* was the enemy. "Strategically, Octavia's right that your magic's a wild card. The smart thing to do would be to work with Bridget and take you out. But I can't do that."

"So you want us to team up against Bridget to take *her* out." My throat tightened, and I could barely get the words out. "You want to kill her."

"I don't like it, either," he said. "But it's our only choice."

"No," I challenged. "It's not *my* only choice."

Sometime while we'd been talking, we'd inched so close to each other that I could feel the heat coming off his skin. His being so close did all sorts of crazy things to my heart, lungs, and head that I felt dizzy standing there.

I tried to force myself to breathe steadily, but it was impossible. My cheeks heated, and I knew they were betraying me by turning pink.

He actually had the nerve to reach his hand up and brush his thumb lightly upon my cheek. He took a sharp breath inward, like that small touch shook him to the core.

Sparks flew through me. Not the angry kind—the *happy* kind. And as much as I knew I should, I couldn't move away.

"You wouldn't be able to kill me, either," he murmured. "Deny it all you want. But I know it's true."

Something wet fell down my cheek. A tear.

He caught it in his finger, and I wanted so badly to throw myself into his arms and let him comfort me. If a single touch made me feel like this, what would it feel like to be wrapped in his arms? To kiss him again?

Our lips were so close. Just a few millimeters more…

No. I pulled away, breaking the contact between us. Coldness swarmed my body. *He's using me, just like he did back at the fountain. We're not soulmates. We're enemies. And I can't ever let myself forget that.*

"You're right. I don't want to kill you," I said, wiping another tear off my cheek. "I don't want to kill *anyone*."

The lump in my throat refused to go away. If I didn't leave now, I was going to completely break down in front of him.

I couldn't let him see that. I couldn't let him comfort me again. Who knew what would happen between us if I did?

Instead, I did the same thing I had last night.

I ran.

But not without hearing his final words before I made it inside the villa.

"I meant everything I said, Selena," he said, his words following me as they carried through the yard. "And I'll be right here tomorrow, waiting for you. Because we're going to work together. It's the best chance we have of making it through this week alive."

30

TORRENCE

KING DEVIN ORDERED us to remain inside our hotel rooms until we were fetched to join him at dinner. He said it was for our own safety. I didn't believe it, but since we needed information from him, we did as he asked.

It was difficult to sleep that night, not knowing what he might have in store for us. I had to keep reminding myself that our kingdoms were allies. Any move against us would be a move against Avalon. And while King Devin was a snake, he wasn't stupid enough to start a war he would most definitely lose.

The next morning, I did the best workout I could manage given the small space and no equipment. The workout was a challenge, because I hadn't had anything to eat since that bite of bread in Utopia, but I managed.

Suddenly, someone knocked on the door.

I sprung up from the floor mid push-up and glanced at my watch. There were hours before dinner.

What was going on?

Maybe King Devin had decided to be generous and let us break bread over lunch instead of dinner? I *hoped* so, but I doubted it.

"Who is it?" I asked, inching cautiously toward the door.

The person on the other side swung the door open, and I was overwhelmed by the metallic scent of vampire.

A beautiful woman with perfectly curled dark hair sashayed inside. She flaunted every curve of her body in a tight white dress that barely covered her butt. Her stilettos were so tall that they looked like they might snap at any second, and she was dripping in diamonds.

Behind her, a mini entourage of similarly dressed vampires rolled in carts upon carts of clothes, makeup, jewelry, and various other items.

"I'm Princess Daniela." The woman appraised me, scrunching her nose at the sight of my Avalon training uniform, sneakers, and hair thrown up into a messy ponytail. "King Devin sent me to prepare you for dinner."

"But dinner isn't for a few hours," I said.

"Exactly," she said. "And now that I'm getting a look at you, I wish he'd sent me earlier." She turned to her entourage, who stood quietly behind her, waiting for her command. "Let's get started immediately," she said. "Because we have a *lot* of work to do."

"Getting ready for dinner" meant a manicure, pedicure, highlights, hair extensions, lash extensions, lip injections, a full face of makeup, and my hair styled with a weird apparatus that sucked my hair around it to dry it into curls.

Princess Daniela lounged on the settee near the window, sipping from a glass of blood as she oversaw the process. She was already on her third glass, which was nearly as much blood as a vampire needed to survive a *day*. She would be drunk on it if she had much more.

"Is all this stuff really necessary?" I asked after drinking the potion that healed my newly plump lips in seconds.

"Of course it is," Princess Daniela said. "King Devin won't stand for an *ungroomed* woman sitting at his dining room table."

"Do you purposefully refer to all women like we're horses?" I snapped.

"The women of the Tower are thoroughbreds." She smiled sweetly, not missing a beat. "We're the best of the best. A properly groomed woman is far more alluring than a man could ever be. Why wouldn't we take care of ourselves and use our beauty to our advantage?"

"I don't know." I shrugged. "Maybe a little something called *respect?*"

"Why do you assume we don't respect ourselves?" There was an edge to her voice, like she was warning me to watch my mouth.

But after being poked and prodded by brushes, tweezers, and needles, my patience had worn thin a while ago.

"You prance around this place like candy on display, waiting to be devoured," I said. "You let the men treat you like objects instead of people. That's lack of self-respect if I've ever seen it."

"On the contrary," she said. "We use our beauty to entrance men into catering to our every whim. And you best take a lesson from us, if you want King Devin to provide you with what you've come here to get."

"Who says we're here to get something from him?"

She downed the final sips of blood from her glass, not bothering to answer the question. "Let's pick your dress." She stood up and strode over to the rack full of tiny dresses, perusing them and sizing me up. "The more it shows off your figure, the better. Because if you can distract the king with your beauty, he'll barely notice when he gives you whatever it is that you desire."

31

TORRENCE

PRINCESS DANIELA WALKED me to King Devin's quarters, and I pulled at the bottom of the skintight red dress she'd insisted I wear. Not that there was much on the bottom to pull at. It felt like my butt was hanging out. The hair extensions literally made my hair longer than the dress.

The top of the dress wasn't much better. It dipped so low that my boobs—which were bound in a push up bra so tight that it might as well have been a corset—were about to pop out. They were accentuated with a diamond drop necklace that fell right between them.

The only things I liked about the outfit were the ankle boots. They were black with red bottoms, and covered with silver studs. I'd insisted on wearing them the moment I'd seen them, since pumps *so* weren't my style. And after enspelling them with the charm Aunt Bella had taught me to make any shoe comfortable, their stilettos were as easy to walk in as sneakers.

As I walked down the hall, I straightened my shoulders, pretending I was on a runway. All I needed were fluffy wings to feel like a Victoria's Secret model. *I'm wearing this outfit, whether I like it or not*, I told myself. *I might as well rock it.*

Princess Daniela led me inside King Devin's quarters and down the hall, stopping at a closed door. "This is where I'm leaving you." She pulled some of my new, long hair over my shoulder and gave me a small smile. "You look stunning. I have no doubt that whatever you're searching for, you'll succeed in getting."

"Thanks," I said, shell-shocked. Had the ice princess just given me a compliment?

"King Devin will be arriving in ten minutes," she said. "Good luck." With that, she opened the doors to the dining room and motioned for me to enter.

Reed, Thomas, and Sage were already sitting at the long table. They all turned to look at me as I stepped inside. I barely heard Princess Daniela close the door behind me.

"Wow." Reed stared at me, his eyes wandering over every inch of my body like he was seeing me for the first time.

It was the longest he'd looked at me, *ever.*

Irritation coursed through me, and I balled my hands into fists. It shouldn't have taken a tight red dress for Reed to finally notice my existence.

Even more irritating was that maybe Princess Daniela was right, and all it took to get a guy to fawn over you was a tight dress, a push-up bra, and a pair of tall, flashy heels.

"Why don't you take a picture?" I said with a fake-sweet smile. "It'll last longer."

"Sorry." He opened his mouth and then closed it, apparently speechless. "You just look different. That's all."

I rolled my eyes. "Don't get used to it," I said as I strutted over to the only empty chair at the table that wasn't the one at the head of it. My long hair swished behind me, making every movement feel bigger and bolder. "I'll be back in my normal clothes the moment we leave this god-awful place tonight."

"Me, too," Sage said from across the table. Her makeover wasn't *nearly* as extreme as mine. Her black dress was as tight and tiny, but other than that, she looked the same. No insanely long hair extensions or plumped up lips. "I've always loved heels, but these feel like they might break my ankles."

"I have a spell to fix that," I said.

"Bella's spell?" She perked up.

Right. Sage and Aunt Bella were friends.

"Yeah," I said. "It'll only take a minute. Put your feet up on the table." There was a lot of space between each of our seats, so she could easily avoid hitting her place setting.

"Reed—turn away," Sage said as she swung her feet up onto the pristine marble table. "Because this dress is *short,* and I'm not wearing much under it."

Thomas gave Reed a warning look, and Reed did as asked.

At least the arrogant mage knew how to show a *bit* of respect. Although it was probably more out of respect for Thomas than for Sage.

But I was done thinking about him. It was time for a bit of fun.

"All right." I rubbed my hands together and focused on Sage's tall, silk stilettos. "This won't take long."

I kept my voice low as I chanted the Latin, my power rising and swirling within me. The purple magic released from my hands, forming into two orbs that floated in my palms. I continued chanting, weaving the details of the spell into the magic in preparation to push it toward Sage's shoes.

Just then, the door swung open, and King Devin stood at the entrance wearing a suit jacket that looked like it was spun from pure gold. I jumped, and the magic flew right out of my hands.

It ricocheted off the window and sunk into King Devin's chest. His entire jacket glowed purple, and the magic disappeared into it.

Crap.

Sage swung her legs off the table, and I lowered my hands to my sides. All four of us sat straight, ready to defend ourselves against a possible attack.

King Devin said nothing. He just stayed where he was and readjusted his jacket.

"Hmm," he said, pulling at the jacket again.

Was that a good hmm or a bad hmm? Definitely a bad one. Why was I even thinking about it? I'd just flung a ball of magic at the king. I didn't know why he hadn't attacked me already. He technically could have, and claimed it was in self-defense.

I was so totally screwed.

Thomas stood and rested his hand on the back of his chair. "Your Highness," he said, bowing his head slightly. "Apologies for the ruckus."

King Devin stared Thomas down.

Then he laughed.

"Sir?" Thomas questioned.

"I just walked inside to a glorious display of your wife's figure upon my table, and a spell that made my favorite jacket fit like a glove." He pulled at the cuffs, looking pleased. "It's one of a kind, as it's woven with strands of Arachne's silk web. My tailor could never get it to fit quite right. But that magic seems to have done the trick." He looked to me, sheer curiosity in his eyes. "Tell me, dear," he said. "How did you do it?"

I sat there, shocked, before realizing that everyone was waiting for me to speak. "It's a spell created by my Aunt Bella," I said quickly. "To make any shoe as comfortable as a sneaker."

"I see." He raised his chin. "A very practical spell. But this jacket is woven with mythical silk. It can't be affected by magic."

"That's the thing about the spell," I said. "It doesn't change anything. The shoes—well, jacket, in your case—remain the same. It's only your perception of how it feels that changes. I guess you could say that the spell isn't actually *on* the jacket. It's *around* it."

"And this spell will remain around the jacket forever?"

"No," I said. "It only lasts for one wear."

"Pity." He frowned. "I'll have to have you teach it to my head witch, so she can perform the spell after you leave."

I bit my lip. Aunt Bella would *not* be happy with my sharing one of our coolest family spells. Only powerful witches could create spells to begin with, and those spells were most always kept within the family—or circle, depending on how close the circle was.

But King Devin had made a demand, not a request. And given the situation, I was sure Aunt Bella would understand.

"Will do," I said, and King Devin looked pleased once more.

"I'll be sure my head witch keeps the spell a secret," he said. "I know how dramatic you witches can be about keeping your spells in the family."

I tensed, saying nothing. How was he able to insult people, be respectful, and shut them down all at once?

"Now," he said, making his way to the chair at the head of the table. "We have much to discuss, and we'll get to that later. Because first... we dine."

32

SELENA

JULIAN IGNORED me the next day. So did Bridget. Julian and Bridget ignored each other, too.

It was safe to say that our alliance of four was officially broken up.

Luckily, I still had Cassia.

"Felix has been in Octavia's suite all day." Cassia frowned, glaring at the stairs. "What are the two of them *doing* up there?"

I had a pretty good idea of what they were doing. I also knew Cassia didn't want to hear about it.

"You know the only reason he's on your mind is because of his magic," I said. "Right?"

"I don't know." She pressed her lips together, her eyes troubled. "We talk sometimes. We *get* each other. I know you don't believe me. But it's true."

She was right. I didn't believe her.

Because if she was right and Felix wasn't using his magic on her, I had a feeling she'd be more concerned about my going to arena this week than about Felix spending most of his time alone with Octavia.

She stopped talking about Felix after that, apparently not wanting to face the fact that he was using his magic on her.

I *so* badly wanted to talk to her about what was happening between Julian and me. But Cassia was a hopeless romantic. If I confided in her, I knew what she'd say.

Go to Julian tonight.

I didn't want to be influenced one way or the other. So I didn't bring it up.

The decision was mine, and mine alone.

And I was still torn on what I wanted to do.

Knowing that Julian was in the back yard waiting for me, I couldn't have slept that night even if I'd tried.

I held out for a bit. But eventually, I couldn't take it anymore. Julian had done as promised and gotten me to create bolts on command.

It would be stupid of me to turn down his help.

At least, that's what I told myself as I sneaked out of my room, unable to stop thinking about how close we'd come to kissing last night.

He was waiting right where he'd promised, and he smirked when he saw me. The glow of the moon shined upon his perfectly sculpted face and dark blond hair. He was way too tempting for his own good.

Well, for *my* own good.

"I knew you'd come," he said once I reached him.

"This doesn't mean I've agreed to team up with you in the arena this week," I said, even though I knew in my heart that was a lie. "But I *do* want to get better at using my magic."

"Smart," he said. "Not like I'm surprised."

I tilted my head playfully. "Are you complimenting me or yourself?"

"Both," he said, and despite not wanting him to believe I *enjoyed* our time together, I gave him a small smile. "Now, let's get to work."

I was officially hopeless.

"Come on," Julian goaded. "You're in the Otherworld because of me. You'll likely die because of me. You *hate* me. Harness that hate. Feel it. *Relish* in it."

I tried. Trust me, I tried. I replayed every moment I'd spent with Julian, starting from when I first saw him at the end of Torrence's driveway. I tried to harness each moment, thinking one might make me angrier than the others.

When he'd kissed me, even though it was all an act.

When he'd dragged me through that portal.

When he'd run away with the bag of money.

The memories hurt. And yes, they made me angry. They made sparks flare to life within me and electricity rush through my skin.

But there were no bolts.

Because I wasn't *as* angry as I'd been before his apology last night. Now that I was thinking about it, he hadn't been anything but kind to me since we were selected for the Faerie Games. And I was truly grateful that he was spending his time helping me when he could be resting up for the arena.

Not like I was *ever* going to give him the satisfaction of admitting it.

Three hours later, I was sweating and burnt out. I hung my arms to my sides in defeat. "This isn't working," I said, grabbing the bottle of water that Julian had thankfully remembered to bring out with him. "Maybe we should stop for the night and try again tomorrow."

"We only have one night after this one before the fight," he said.

"I know, I know." I sat down on the ground, too tired to stand.

He plopped down right next to me.

For a few seconds, we sat there in companionable silence.

Even though I felt burnt out from calling so much electricity into my body, his being so close to me made the sparks flare up once again.

I shouldn't have been thinking about my attraction to Julian when there were so many other important, serious matters to deal with. But my body constantly betrayed me around him. I pulled my legs up to my chest and wrapped my arms around them, as if I could put out the flames within me.

It didn't work.

"You're really okay with this?" I finally asked, needing to somehow break the silence.

"Okay with what?"

"With the fact that Bridget will most likely die in the arena on Friday." I could barely say it. I could barely bring myself to *think* about it. But I couldn't ignore it, either.

"Of course I'm not okay with it." He turned to look at

me, his eyes shining with sheer honesty. "Especially because I'll be the one who does it."

"We'll be working together," I said. "We'll *both* be the ones who do it."

"But I'm taking the killing blow."

I opened my mouth to protest, but no words came out. Because I didn't *want* to take the killing blow. When the time came, I knew I wouldn't be able to do it.

"I'm going to do it as quickly and painlessly as possible," he said. "She'll be gone before even realizing what happened."

That shouldn't have been comforting.

But somehow, it was.

I said nothing. What was there to say? Instead, I just sat there, unable to look away from his intense, raw gaze.

He might not have said it out loud, but his decision to be the one to take out Bridget was tearing him up inside. His struggle swirled within me, almost like it was my own. And when my elbow unintentionally touched his, comforting warmth made its way through my entire body.

He didn't move away. Neither did I.

Without realizing I was doing it, my eyes traveled to his lips. *There might not be anything to say to make this better,* I thought. *But there is something I can do...*

My breathing slowed. His did, too. It was like we were both in a trance. I kept moving forward, and the next thing I knew, my lips brushed lightly against his.

He stilled, and I worried that I'd done something wrong. But then his arm was around my back, and he pulled me up onto his lap, his tongue parting my lips and connecting with mine.

I let out a soft moan, sinking into him and kissing him back with everything in me. Our bodies fit together perfectly. He was warm and loving, and in his arms, my mind turned to mush. There was no magic practice session, there were no Faerie Games, and there was no arena fight to worry about. There was only Julian, and there was only knowing that in this moment, everything felt right.

My hand ran down his body, needing to explore every inch of him. The soft skin of his cheek, his perfectly sculpted chest, and his hard, defined abs. His hands tangled through my hair, sending warm tingles deep into my stomach and leaving me wanting *more*.

With no space left between us, the kiss intensified, until somehow, I was on the ground with him on top of me. We moved together like a dance, perfectly in tandem. Every inch of my skin buzzed with excitement. On instinct, my hand lowered even farther, until it was just above his hip—the same location as my clover birthmark.

Suddenly, he pulled himself off of me, and his expression hardened. Whatever he'd felt a few seconds before—if he'd felt anything at all—was gone.

I breathed shallowly, the warmth sucked out of me as I sat up as well. How was he so close one moment, and so far away the next? Had he felt anything I'd felt? Or had I just been a pretty girl throwing myself at him, bringing his primal instincts to the surface?

The thought, along with the cold way he was looking at me, made me lower my head in shame.

"We should head back and get some sleep," he said coldly. "We're both tired, and you fried yourself out. We'll return to practicing tomorrow night, once we're thinking clearly again."

He stood, not reaching out a hand to help me up. It was like the sheer thought of touching me disgusted him.

I pushed myself off the ground and wiped the dirt off the back of my ridiculously skimpy fighting outfit. But I straightened out the skirt, wanting to look as unruffled as he did.

As we silently walked back, he made sure to walk a few steps ahead of me. Heated sparks rose up in me again. Not from anger, and definitely not from happiness.

This time, they were from the deep embarrassment of rejection.

33

SELENA

DINNER the next night was the same as every other dinner since Octavia had become Empress of the Villa.

It was taken over by Octavia and her followers.

A line had been drawn in the sand, and it was a *visible* line when we all sat at the dining room table. Octavia sat at the head of it, and her crew surrounded her. Pierce, Emmet, Antonia, and Felix.

Julian, Cassia, Bridget, and I sat at the opposite end. None of us really spoke to each other through the meals. Cassia made a few attempts, but they were futile.

In the middle of the two groups was Cillian. It didn't seem like anyone knew where his head was at.

"I've got a secret," Pierce said mysteriously once the desserts appeared. His voice echoed loudly through the room, bringing the attention where he liked it most—on himself. "And I think *everyone* at this table will be interested in hearing it."

We all looked to him. The orbs circled around him, too.

He grinned, relishing in the attention.

What a camera-whore. He was just as bad as Emmet.

He rubbed his hands together, smirking as he met all of our eyes. He made sure to smirk at the orbs around him, too.

He took a deep breath, looked at me, and said, "Selena can't create lightning bolts at will."

Octavia snickered from the head of the table.

"That's not true," I lied.

"It *is* true," Pierce insisted. "Someone saw you practicing last night. A trusted source. They watched you try and fail to create bolts—repeatedly. You can't do it."

I glanced around everyone sitting around the table. Who could have been spying on me and Julian?

No one met my eyes. Not even Julian.

Did Julian sell me out to Pierce?

My heart dropped. I didn't want to believe it—even though it seemed to be the most likely scenario.

"I *can* do it." Heat sparked through my veins, and I held Pierce's haughty gaze. "Everyone at this table—no, everyone watching the *Games*—has seen me create bolts. Or did you forget the Magic Demonstration Ceremony?

The arena fight where Molly was murdered?" Anger rose in my voice, and I braced my palms on the top of the table. "The Emperor of the Villa competition a few days ago?"

"I remember them all," Pierce said. "You didn't create those bolts at will. They just shot out of you, wild and uncontrolled. *You're* uncontrolled."

Octavia sat back and crossed her legs, looking at me in amusement. "This is why I selected you to go to the arena this week," she said. "You're dangerous." She glanced around at everyone sitting around the table, staring at them until they had no choice but to meet her gaze. "If any of you don't see how dangerous she is, you're an idiot, and you deserve to go to the arena next."

Electricity flooded my body. Everyone disappeared into the background—all I saw were bright flashes of white, mixed with blue magic.

A second later, the brightness subsided.

The table—and everything that had been on it—was gone. All that was left was a pile of ashes on the intricately woven rug.

Everyone remained in their seats. Some of the champions still held their utensils in their hands. They all looked at me in shock, and the orbs flew around me excitedly.

"I didn't mean to," I mumbled, watching the ashes

rise and re-form themselves into the table. Less than a minute later, everything was the same as it had been before. Even the food and drinks had been restored.

"Exactly," Octavia said. "You didn't mean to. *That's* the problem."

Pierce looked at Bridget, and then at Julian. "If the two of you know what's good for you, you'll team up tomorrow and take Selena out," he said. "Get back into the good graces of the rest of us in the villa. We'll definitely owe you safety if you pull through on this one. At least for a week or two."

Heat flooded through me, rushing straight to my cheeks. I stood up and slammed my hands onto the table. It shook so hard that the lighter objects jumped, some of them going straight off the ledge.

"I don't know who this 'source' of yours is," I said, zeroing in on Pierce. "But he or she didn't see everything that happened last night."

That was an understatement.

Because whoever this source was had failed to mention that I wasn't practicing alone. I looked around at everyone suspiciously.

What's their angle?

Octavia raised an eyebrow. "Are you planning on filling in the blanks?" she asked calmly, like she didn't care if I did or didn't.

"You wish." I stood straighter and gave her a hateful glare of my own. "But whoever went to Pierce, I hope you come to me tonight." I spoke slower and more intensely, making a point of meeting all the eyes at the table.

None of them looked away. Any one of them could be Pierce's source.

And I wanted to know why his source hadn't mentioned that I was practicing with Julian.

"You'll find I'm surprisingly good at listening," I said, throwing my napkin on the table to signify that I was done. "Because I prefer being stabbed in the front than in the back."

34

SELENA

AFTER DINNER, I retreated to the library with Cassia, like I had every night since Octavia had become Empress of the Villa. Cassia told me stories of the Otherworld, and I told her stories of Avalon. I also told her about Earth, since I knew a fair share about it from the books, movies, and television shows I watched that came to Avalon from Earth.

No one bothered us in the library, since they were too busy sucking up to Octavia in her suite.

But we'd only been chatting for fifteen minutes before there was a knock on the door.

My heart leaped, and Cassia and I looked at each other in surprise.

I leaned back in my armchair in an attempt to look

calm. "Come in," I said, making sure my voice didn't shake.

The door creaked open, and Julian walked inside, followed by Felix. Felix shut the door as quickly as possible behind him.

I sat straighter. *Since when are Julian and Felix friends?*

"Hi, guys." I looked back and forth between them, trying to hide my confusion. "What's going on?"

"Felix came to me while we were both in the bath-house," Julian said. "He has an interesting proposition he wants to make."

I turned my focus to Felix, saying nothing as I waited for him to speak.

"I'm the one who saw you practicing last night," Felix cut straight to the chase. "Or should I say, I saw the *two* of you practicing." He looked pointedly at Julian, and then back at me.

"You're Pierce's source," I said.

He nodded, although I already knew it was true.

"Why'd you do it?" I stood and looked at him head on, wanting us to be closer to the same level. Felix was taller than me, but it was better than nothing. "If you were going to rat me out to Pierce, why not take Julian down with me?"

"Because now Pierce thinks I'm his little lapdog." Felix

sneered. "But it was never his trust I wanted to build. It was yours." He looked away from me to glance at Julian, and then at Cassia. His gaze lingered on hers for a moment too long, and her porcelain cheeks turned pink. "All of yours."

I *so* badly wanted to roll my eyes and walk out on him. But earlier at dinner, I'd said I was open to listening. Sticking to my word was important. So I needed to at least hear him out. What did I have to lose?

Julian gave me a single nod, like he was proud of me for thinking before reacting. My heart swelled, and I hated myself for it.

But Felix was the one I was concerned with right now. Not Julian. And so, I turned my attention back to him.

"Ratting me out was a terrible way to try earning my trust," I said. "But get talking."

"I have no official alliances in the Games." Felix spoke quickly, like he knew my patience was wearing thin. "The other guys—and probably Antonia, too—will send me to the arena without thinking twice if they get Emperor of the Villa."

"Even Pierce?" I asked.

"Maybe not yet," he said. "But at the end of the day, Pierce's allegiance is with Emmet and the others."

I pursed my lips, since that much was obvious given

the comfortable way Pierce and Emmet interacted with each other. They were a duo.

Which meant they needed to be broken up, quickly.

"So you want an alliance with us," I guessed.

"You got it."

Cassia stood up from the couch and brought her hair around her shoulders. "It's a good idea," she said, staring at Felix with her wide, doe-like eyes. "Especially since we'll need someone to replace Bridget."

I gave her a sharp look. "We don't know for sure what will happen in the arena tomorrow."

She bit her lip, like she wanted to say something but was holding back.

Felix actually had the nerve to chuckle. "You and Julian were practicing together last night," he said. "You're clearly planning to work together to take out Bridget."

My chest panged, and I said nothing. The truth of it was too terrible to speak out loud.

"What does Bridget have to say about all of this?" Felix continued in that annoyingly mocking way of his.

"Nothing," I said. "She's avoided talking to us all week."

"So she knows."

I stiffened and pressed my lips together. Because one

of Bridget's gifts was prophecy. Of course she knew. And the fact that she was avoiding us terrified me.

What does she have planned?

"Let's say you're right that Selena and I are working together." Julian's steely gaze was fixed on Felix. "What do you have to offer us?"

Felix's lips curved up into a small smile. "Perhaps we should sit down?" He motioned to the couches.

"No," I said. "I prefer to remain standing."

"All right, then." He took a deep breath and rubbed his hands together. "The three of you have strong magic," he started. "But your strength is mostly physical. What I offer the team is something different—something the three of you *need*. Mental magic. The ability to coax other players to do my bidding."

"Only the females," I was quick to retort.

"Most of them," he corrected, and I narrowed my eyes at him, trying to will him into silence about my immunity to his magic. "But yes. My magic works on all of the females who aren't in our alliance."

Julian looked at Felix with interest. "It doesn't work on the ones in our alliance?" he asked.

I stared at Felix harder. *Don't tell him*, I thought. *Say nothing, and maybe you'll gain a bit of my trust.*

It was stupid, really. Because Julian *wasn't* my soulmate.

But I still didn't want him to know about my immunity to Felix's magic.

"I never said that," Felix said. "But I won't use my magic against my allies. At least not until the four of us are the only ones left in the Games. *If* you take me up on my offer, of course."

I relaxed slightly. That might not have been much, but it was a start.

Maybe Felix was worth teaming up with, after all. But there was one big catch.

"Do you think you can use your magic to help us take Octavia down?" I asked.

"I know I can." He smirked. "I've spent every night with her in her suite this week. She's in love with me already."

"And you feel the same about her?" Cassia broke in, frowning.

Felix's eyes softened as he gazed at Cassia. "Of course not," he said, his voice calm and reassuring. "I wouldn't be in here proposing an alliance to the three of you if I were."

Cassia continued to gaze up at him, like she wanted it to be true, but also wasn't sure if she should believe him. "So why spend so much time with her?" she asked.

"To make sure she didn't send me to the arena this week," he said. "And it worked."

"It did," I said, and while Cassia agreed as well, she didn't look pleased. "So, you have Octavia under your control. Assuming you're not in an alliance with her—"

"I'm not," he said with so much force that I couldn't help but think he was telling the truth. "Octavia might want to protect me in the Games, but I don't intend to do the same for her."

"Let's say I believe you," I said. "How exactly do you plan to use your influence over Octavia to help us take her out?"

"I'm glad you asked." He smiled. "Because the next time one of the three of you wins Emperor of the Villa, I assume you're going to send Octavia to the arena again."

"That's the plan," Julian said.

"Good." Felix's expression turned more serious than it had since he'd first entered the room. "Because I want you to send me in there with her."

"What?" I sputtered. "You can't be serious."

"We won't do it." Cassia crossed her arms, standing her ground. "At least, *I* won't do it."

Julian stepped forward, and all eyes went to him. "We can, and we will," he said, and the orbs buzzed around him, eating up his every word. "And we'll send someone much stronger than her in there with the two of them. Someone who isn't in Octavia's alliance. Cillian."

"My thoughts exactly," Felix said, turning his attention back to Cassia and me. "It's sweet that the two of you want to protect me, it really is—"

"Don't flatter yourself," I cut him off, scowling. "All I said was that your proposition is crazy."

"It's not crazy," he said. "It benefits me long term."

"How so?"

"Because Octavia won't fight me," he said confidently. "Which means she'll fight Cillian. Cillian's stronger than Octavia, and he won't take kindly to her attacking him. They'll fight, Cillian will win, and *boom*. Octavia's taken care of, I'll earn protection and trust from the three of you, and we'll plow our way straight to the final four."

"So you're offering yourself as a pawn."

"I am," he said. "In return for your loyalty for the rest of the Games."

He exuberated excitement, and I glanced at Julian and Cassia. Cassia was hanging onto Felix's every word. Julian was much harder to read.

"It's a solid offer," Julian finally said. "If we accept, do you promise to stop using your magic on Selena and Cassia?"

"Yes," Felix said. "I promise."

Julian nodded, apparently satisfied, and turned to me. "What do you think?" he asked.

The three of them watched me expectantly. I

couldn't believe this. If someone had told me last week that I'd be considering an alliance with Felix, I would have thought they were nuts.

I also wouldn't have thought that we'd be forced to turn on Bridget so soon. But here we were. And I needed to do whatever was necessary to keep myself, Julian, and Cassia alive until the Nephilim army found its way into the Otherworld and put an end to this.

"To the final four," I said, putting my hand in the center of our circle.

"To the final four," Felix said, adding his hand into the center. He was followed by Julian and Cassia.

And just like that, our new alliance was formed.

35

TORRENCE

I'D MENTALLY prepared myself for a drawn-out, multi-course meal.

Luckily, it was only three courses. A soup, a giant steak, and a caramel flan for dessert.

We were served by scantily clad human women, and from their sickly pale complexions, they clearly also served as snacks for the vampires of the Tower. I wished I could do something to help them, but overthrowing the entire kingdom of the Tower unfortunately wasn't on our agenda today.

The steak was as delicious as King Devin had claimed it would be. And after having not eaten for over twenty-four hours, we devoured every last bite of it.

It was easy to remember the Tower's rule that

women should only speak when spoken to when I was busy eating such mouth-watering food.

The wine was delicious as well, although we made sure to only drink enough to be polite. We needed our heads clear for the discussion we were about to have with the king.

King Devin made polite conversation throughout the meal, mainly with Thomas. He rarely directed any questions toward me or Sage, and Reed wasn't a talkative guy. So we all ended up hearing about how Thomas and Sage had met when Sage was young, and weren't reunited until many years later. Sage even blushed a few times, sharing a few knowing glances with Thomas as he recounted the story about how they'd been torn apart multiple times, but love ended up winning in the end.

"I seem to have taken over the conversation with all this prattle," Thomas said after describing his and Sage's wedding. "What about you? Do you still visit the faerie princess you met at the crossroads?"

The king's eyes darkened, and my hand froze right before digging my spoon into another bite of flan.

Wrong question.

"No," the king said, his voice clipped. "A few years after we fell in love, she met her soulmate. I haven't gone to her since."

Awkward silence descended upon the table.

"This dessert is delicious," I said, needing to say something to clear the air.

"Is it a specialty of the region?" Sage sounded *way* more bubbly than usual.

"It is," he said, apparently so relieved about the change of subject that he wasn't even angry at us for speaking out of turn. "I'm glad you're enjoying it."

From there, Thomas shifted the conversation back to more pleasant, mundane topics.

Finally, the servers cleared our plates and brought us each a cup of coffee called *tetero*. I'd never loved the taste of coffee, but this one was tolerable, since it had far more hot milk than espresso.

"Now," King Devin said once the servers left us alone with our coffee. "It's time to get down to business."

I immediately perked up, my knees bouncing as I waited for him to continue.

"I have four matching items in my possession that will transport you directly to the Otherworld," he said. "But like I told you last night, I won't give these items to you for free."

"What's the price?" Reed asked.

King Devin smirked, and I had a feeling we weren't going to like what was coming. "I require that you bring me four specific items," he said. "The hide of the

Nemean lion, Circe's staff, Aphrodite's girdle, and the egg of a phoenix."

We were all silent for a few seconds. Was he crazy?

"Those items don't exist," Sage said what we were surely all thinking.

"I enjoyed you much more when you had your legs spread out on my table." King Devin sighed and glanced at her breasts. He'd been staring at our cleavage a lot through the meal, and I had to swallow down disgust each time. "Your ignorance is shining through, my dear."

Sage snarled, and the tips of her fingers shifted into claws under the table.

A huge part of me wanted to watch her shred the king's smirk right off his face. But the other part—the logical part—knew that wouldn't get us anywhere.

Sage knew the same thing, because her claws quickly shifted back into human form.

"My wife is correct," Thomas said firmly. "Those items are myths. We can't bring you things that don't exist."

"What exactly is a 'myth?'" King Devin leaned back in his chair, brought his thumb to his chin, and studied us all. "Some would say the Holy Grail is a myth. Many would claim that Excalibur is a myth. Yet, you have both of those items at Avalon. Do you not?"

"We do," I said, and Thomas gave me a *look* to remind me that I was speaking out of turn.

But King Devin just gave me a knowing smile. "Why are the items I listed any different?" he asked.

I pressed my lips together, since he made a good point.

"Your jacket," Reed said suddenly, his gaze boring down upon the king. "You said it was made with threads from Arachne's silk web. And Arachne's from Greek mythology, just like the objects you requested we bring to you."

"Ah." King Devin sat straighter to take another sip of his coffee. "I'm glad one of you was paying attention earlier."

I scowled, because of course we'd all heard the king say his jacket was made with threads from Arachne's web. I just hadn't believed him. I'd assumed he'd been tricked into paying a hefty price for something spelled by an extraordinarily strong witch.

"I'm sure your jacket is one of a kind," Thomas said delicately. "But can you prove it's truly woven with Arachne's silk?"

"It's indestructible." He removed the jacket and tossed it onto the center of the table. "Do what you want with it. Nothing will harm it."

"Reed has the most powerful magic of all of us,"

Thomas said. "If anyone can test to see if the jacket is a forgery, it's him."

"Perfect," the king said. "If your mage destroys the jacket, I'll give you the four items that will take you to the Otherworld right now. If he doesn't, then you'll seek out the objects I requested and only return when you can deliver them to me in exchange for the items that will take you to the Otherworld."

"Deal." Reed stood up and studied the jacket, his dark eyes as intense and focused as ever. Unlike a witch, he didn't need to chant a spell to bring his magic to the surface. He just raised his arms and shot a beam of bright yellow magic out of his palms. His dark eyes glowed, and in that moment, he looked truly terrifying.

But nothing happened to the jacket. His magic didn't seem to touch it.

Reed cursed and threw his magic simultaneously toward two silver candlesticks that were also on the table. They shattered on the spot.

He shot another beam of magic toward the jacket, but this time, he held it for longer. He pushed more and more magic into the beam, and it pulsed with the intensity of his power.

No matter how hard he tried, the jacket remained unaffected. It *absorbed* the magic.

Whatever material the jacket was made of was more powerful than a mage.

Reed grunted, sweat dripping from his brow as he forced even *more* power into his magic. Then he stopped. He flexed his fingers and dropped his arms to his sides. "I can't do it," he admitted, sitting back down and refusing to look at any of us.

"Of course you can't." The king stood up, lifted the jacket off the table, and put it back on. "Ah," he said, wiggling around a bit. "It's back to fitting slightly incorrectly. Do you want to do that spell again?"

He looked to me, and I knew it was a demand instead of a request.

I hated that we were at this disgusting man's mercy.

But I did as he asked, chanting the spell and flinging my purple magic at his chest again.

"Thank you." He smiled and returned to his seat, folding his hands on top of the table. "Would the four of you like to enter into a blood oath to finalize our agreement?"

"We would," Thomas said.

"I assumed so," he said. "I'm a man of my word, so that won't be a problem."

After working out the exact phrasing of the blood oath, we each went through the ritual of slicing our palms, saying the words of the oath, and sealing the deal with the king.

It was official. We weren't allowed to return to the Tower without the four objects King Devin had requested, and he wasn't allowed to refuse to give us the four items that would bring us to the Otherworld once we completed his task.

If any of us went against the oath, that person's blood would turn against them and burn them to death from the inside out.

"I'm glad we were able to reach an agreement." King Devin finished the last of his coffee and dabbed the corner of his lips with his napkin. "Now, I'm sure you're itching to get started. I'll send for my head witch so Torrence can teach her that magnificent spell. Then, Prince Gustavo will see you out so you can be on your way."

36

SELENA

ON THE MORNING of the arena fight, there was only one object in my closet. A slinky gladiator outfit identical to the ones Octavia and Molly had worn last week.

Julian looked as dangerous as ever in his gladiator outfit that left his chest bare. Defined, slender muscles covered nearly every inch of his body. Only his bottom was fully covered by his gold gladiator kilt, which hung low on his hipbones.

If only it dipped an inch or two lower, I'd know he wasn't my soulmate once and for all.

In the carriage ride to the arena, Bridget wouldn't look at Julian or me. Knowing what was about to happen, I couldn't look at her, either.

The way she'd avoided us all week was strange. The champions selected to go to the arena usually made an effort to talk one-on-one, to try making deals. I knew Bridget hadn't come to me, and Julian said she hadn't gone to him, either. I believed him.

Her behavior was sketchy, and being around her put me on edge.

What does she have planned for us in the arena?

We weren't even halfway to the capital before the carriage ride started to feel unbearably long. "Can the fae not teleport?" I mused, gazing out at the endless green hills below us.

"They technically can," Julian said. "But teleporting was banned from the Otherworld back in Queen Gloriana's time. There's a spell over the realm that keeps even the empress herself from teleporting."

"Why?" I asked.

"We love nature," Bridget said quickly. "The act of traveling immerses us into places in the realm we might have never seen otherwise."

"I see." I tried not to make a big deal out of the fact that this was the first time in a week she'd said a word to me. "But what about when something needs to be done quickly?"

"The spell that prohibits teleportation was cast by full fae—not by half-bloods." She shrugged. "Time is different to immortals. A year to us is like a day to them.

There's no need to rush from place to place if you have centuries—even millennia—ahead of you."

At the mention of immortality, her gray eyes darkened.

Goosebumps rose on my arms at the reminder that her hours in our world were most likely numbered.

"Why have you avoided us all week?" I asked now that the conversation between us had opened.

"I received a few visions after Octavia became Empress of the Villa," she said. "Visions that go beyond the scope of the Games."

"What do you mean?"

"I can't tell you." She shook her head, looking truly sad about it. "But there's a specific way the fight needs to pan out today. I've been spending time alone as I come to terms with accepting it."

She turned away, making it clear she didn't want to speak about it further.

We rode the rest of the way to the Coliseum in silence.

Once we arrived, the driver turned the opposite way of the carriages taking the other champions to the Royal Box. We flew down to a modest abode next to the Coliseum. The gates swung open to let us inside, and it turned out not to be a house at all, but a ramped entrance descending into an underground tunnel. The walls of the tunnel were lit with what looked like twinkling Christmas lights.

The path eventually widened into an area of arched passages that appeared to make up the basement of the Coliseum. The walls and floor were bare, and there was no natural light anywhere.

My chest tightened, and I held onto the side of the carriage to steady myself. "We're beneath the fighting pit," I said. "Aren't we?"

"Yes." Julian was tense in his seat beside me. "We are."

As we rolled along the path, we passed cages holding lions and tigers. They growled as our winged horse passed them, licking their lips like they wanted to eat the magnificent creature for breakfast.

Will they be in the arena with us today? I stared into a lion's empty, hungry eyes, and my heart leaped into my throat. *God, I hope not.*

Eventually, we stopped in what I assumed was the center of the arena. Three half-blood men stood in a short line, their arms straight to their sides as our carriage pulled up in front of them. Once we stopped, the man in the center stepped forward and opened the door for us.

"Each of you will come with one of us," he instructed, not meeting any of our eyes. "We'll take you to separate locations and prepare you for your entrance into the arena."

Bridget held her head high, as stoic as ever as she stepped out first. The half-blood ushered her away the moment both of her feet were on the ground.

The next half-blood stepped forward and looked to me, waiting.

This is it. Icy fear froze my bones. I didn't want to follow this strange man into the depths of this cold basement. I wanted to be back home, in Avalon. I could practically smell the tropical air as I pictured the lush island that had once been my prison, and now felt like an unreachable haven.

Suddenly, Julian's warm fingers brushed against my forearm, grounding me back into reality. "It's going to be okay," he murmured in my ear. "I won't let anything happen to you. I promise."

I nodded, believing him. Julian was strong. He was the most skilled in combat of all the champions. He was going to protect me.

And if the fight didn't go as planned…

Electricity sparked to life under my skin, like a comforting web of safety. I flexed my fingers, the magic buzzing through me.

I have the power to protect myself.

I took one final look into Julian's caring blue eyes before stepping out of the carriage.

The moment my feet touched the ground, the half-blood servant grabbed my hand and pulled me into the darkness.

———

It took every ounce of control not to fry the half-blood on the spot as he hurried me through the damp stone hallway.

Breaking the rules means instant death, I reminded myself over and over and over again.

If I died in the Games, it would be at the hands of one of the other champions. Not because I broke the rules and got myself eliminated.

We turned a corner, and ahead of me was a tall, narrow cage standing at the end of the hall. Its door was open, and the half-blood wasted no time hurling me inside of it and locking it closed.

I collided into the cage's hard floor with a thud. But I forced myself to stand, fear lodging in my throat as I gripped the cold metal bars and shook them as hard as I could. They didn't budge.

Terror built in my chest, and my breaths shallowed,

my eyes darting around in panic. I was just like those animals I'd seen earlier, trapped inside of a cage.

But my cage wasn't only the physical one surrounding me. It was the entire Otherworld itself.

"That metal was forged by Vulcan," the half-blood said casually. "He's the only one strong enough to break it."

That didn't stop me from putting all my strength into trying—and failing—to shake it again. I screamed and jolted it with my electricity, but other than a blink of dull light, nothing happened. I screamed again, but this time, I dropped my arms to my sides in defeat.

Expending energy now was stupid and careless. I needed to be strong for the upcoming fight.

"I'm glad you've come to your senses," the half-blood said.

"Why?" I asked. "Are you rooting for me or something?"

"The spell that Juno places upon us during the Games forbids us from telling you our opinions or saying anything that'll help you," he said. "But as Jupiter's first chosen champion, you're certainly intriguing. And I know you don't want to die today."

"So you *are* rooting for me."

"I can't say one way or the other."

However, his mischievous indigo eyes told another

story. The fae were tricky, and good with twisting their words.

He wanted me to win.

"You'll remain here until Bacchus is ready for you," he changed the subject, serious once more.

"Where will I go once he's ready?" I asked.

"You'll be transported to the arena. And then, you'll fight."

SELENA

As I waited for Bacchus, I asked the half-blood about his life. Talking with him didn't quell my anxiety, but it was better than waiting alone.

His name was Rufus. He lived in a tiny insula apartment in the outskirts of the capital with his wife and three children. He was one of the many half-bloods who acted as caretakers to the animals held in the pens under the Coliseum.

The animals were there because on the days when the Coliseum wasn't hosting the Faerie Games, half-bloods came from all over the Otherworld to fight them in the arena. The ones who won received money for their families. The sum depended on how much the viewers enjoyed the show. The ones who lost—and they usually lost—became that animal's next meal.

Rufus was receiving double his hourly wage for the honor of being in charge of me today, instead of doing his usual job of taking care of the animals.

He was telling me about his son's dream to become a wood carver when a loud clang above us cut the conversation short. A beam of bright light flooded into the basement, and it took a second for my eyes to adjust. The cheering and stomping of the crowd roared overhead.

I pressed my face against the bars and twisted around so I could look up. A trap door was open in the ceiling.

It was about the same size as the perimeter of my cage.

"It's time," Rufus said, and what sounded like the rungs of a chain clinked above me.

The cage jolted, and I stumbled backward, holding my arms out to steady myself. I gripped onto the bars as the cage started to rise, meeting Rufus's eyes in fear.

"Your magic is strong." He tilted his neck upward as he watched me ascend. "We've seen you harness that strength. Now, it's up to you to show them how powerful you can be!"

My electricity surged, his words lighting a fire within me.

I can do this.

Rufus technically hadn't said anything I didn't know. Which, I supposed, was why he'd been able to say it. Because he wasn't saying he supported me, or giving me outside information that would help me in the Games.

But still, his words *did* help me. Not on a literal level, but on a mental one.

And if I made it out of the Games alive, I wouldn't forget the support he'd given me today.

38

SELENA

THE CAGE ROSE UP into the edge of the arena. I removed my hands from the bars once I surfaced and stood strong, not wanting to look like a scared, trapped animal.

The floor of the arena was flat and covered in plain, brown dirt. And fire burned around the perimeter. The orange flames must have been three times my height, and they were hot against my back. They crackled and popped so loudly that they dulled the cheering of the crowd.

Julian and Bridget waited in matching cages, although we were all as far apart from each other as possible.

One longsword and one dagger made of black glass —obsidian—lay on the ground in front of each of us.

This seemed like it was going to be far more similar to a traditional gladiator battle than the watery one last week. A fight to the death using swords and knives.

A fight rigged in Julian's favor.

The fae and the gods want Julian and me to take Bridget out of the Games.

Bacchus flew in his chariot overhead, looking as dark and twisted as he had last week. "Champions, get ready!" He pulled on the reins of his jaguars, stopping the chariot so it hovered in the center of the Coliseum. "This fight begins in three, two, ONE!"

Our cage doors popped open.

The tightness in my chest released, and I stepped out onto the ground.

Immediately, I reached down to pick up the sword and the dagger. The obsidian blades were enforced with magic so they wouldn't break, and they were lighter than the steel we used on Avalon.

I held the swords at the ready, balancing on the balls of my feet in preparation to fight. Julian and Bridget did the same. Our cages sank back into the ground, and the trap doors slammed shut.

It was only us, the weapons, and the fire. With the flames burning so high, it was easy to pretend the crowd wasn't even there—as long as I didn't look up.

We all three stared each other down. But no one moved to attack first.

"You can't put this off forever!" Bacchus yelled from above. "We've made sure to see to that!"

He raised his hand, and his purple magic circled around the perimeter of the fighting ground. The fire grew stronger and moved inward. The heat burned into my back, giving me no choice but to hurry forward. If I didn't, the flames would consume me, burning me to death.

The fire pushed us forward, forward, and more forward. Once the center of the arena was half the size it was before, the flames stopped growing.

I glanced at Julian.

He was intensely focused on Bridget, his swords raised.

Bridget stared back at him, also in fighting position.

I might as well have been invisible to them both.

You're skilled with a blade, I told myself. *If you attack now, you can take Bridget by surprise. A clean swing straight through the neck, making it as instantaneous as possible.*

But I couldn't kill her in cold blood.

I wasn't a murderer.

Then, Julian looked over at me. His pained expression said it all.

He wasn't a murderer, either.

The crowd roared in discontent, screaming at us to fight. Their cries turned into an anthem. *Fight, fight, FIGHT!*

Suddenly, Bridget raced toward Julian, moving in a blur thanks to her super-speed.

He snapped into focus, raising his blades to protect himself. The crowd cheered in excitement, and even the flames burned brighter and higher.

But Julian and Bridget didn't fight.

Because Bridget dropped her weapons and ran straight into his knife.

He stared at her with wide, shocked eyes as she stumbled backward, the knife embedded deep into her stomach. It gave a sickening squish as she removed it. She looked to the bloody blade and dropped it to the ground.

Unable to stand, she fell down next to it.

As she did, she reached for Julian. She grabbed the top of his kilt and pulled it down a few centimeters. Not so far down as to expose him, but far enough to uncover the clover birthmark on his left hipbone.

I dropped both of my weapons to the ground.

Julian was my soulmate.

I didn't know how it was possible. Half-bloods rarely had soulmates. Yet, at the same time, it all made sense. The strange, magnetic pull I felt toward him. The way

I'd inherently trusted him, despite my training on Avalon that told me to always be wary of strangers. The way my entire body warmed whenever he so much as brushed a finger upon my skin. The way everything felt strangely *right* every time we were together. And finally, the way I couldn't bring myself to hate him, despite everything he'd done that had shown me I should.

I think I'd known, somewhere deep in my heart, that we were soulmates. I'd known it from the moment Finn and Bryan had told me about the soulmate bond.

From the intense way Bridget was looking at me, she knew, too. What had just happened hadn't been an accident. She'd revealed his mark to me on purpose.

The question was, what was I going to do about it? Unless the Nephilim army came to rescue us soon, it was impossible for this to end well.

I couldn't imagine my life without Julian in it. And now, I knew why.

But this wasn't the time to figure out where to go from there. Because my friend was bleeding out into the dirt.

I needed to be there for Bridget.

I ran to her side in a flash and put pressure on the wound to slow the bleeding. But it was no use. My hands were the only things keeping her intestines inside of her. The injury was fatal.

Julian must have recovered from his shock, because he stood strong above us, holding his blade high above his head. The fire blazing around us flickered across his face, making him look even more determined to finish what we'd started. "I'll make this quick," he said. "I promise."

"Wait." Bridget held out a hand to stop him. "Please."

He looked to me in question, his blade still raised.

"These are her final moments," I said, not realizing I was crying until I tasted the salt on my tongue. "If she wants us to be here for her, then that's what we'll do."

He nodded and joined me, kneeling onto the bloodied dirt and dropping his sword to the ground.

"Why did you do it?" he asked her. "You could have fought. You could have tried to live. But instead..." He glanced at her stomach, where her blood was slipping past my fingers.

She reached forward, grabbed my top, and pulled me toward her. "You have to win," she said, her breaths so shallow that she could barely get the words out. "The fate of the world depends on it."

Before I could ask what she meant by that, her eyes clouded over. But I could still see her pupils moving underneath the haze.

This wasn't death.

This was a vision.

After about ten seconds, the haze cleared. Her gray eyes were no longer resigned.

They were filled with a newfound determination.

"What did you see?" Julian held onto her shoulder so tightly that it looked like he'd try to shake the answer out of her if she wasn't bleeding out on the ground.

"You're hurting me," she wheezed.

"Sorry." He pulled his hands away, lowering his eyes in shame.

In a flash, she reached for the bloodied knife by her side and thrust it straight toward Julian's heart.

"NO!" White-hot anger shot through me as the thought of a life without Julian sped through my mind.

A bolt of lightning struck down from the sky, hitting Bridget straight in the chest.

The bolt disappeared quickly, but her entire body glowed and buzzed with crawling vines of electricity. She screamed as the electric vines sliced through her skin, her blood vessels blackening and bursting outward from the point where she was struck.

She seized, and then she was still.

Her clothing was singed and curled.

Her eyes—now red from the burst blood vessels—stared blankly up at me.

She was dead.

And the knife had fallen onto the ground in front of Julian.

He was okay. She hadn't gotten to him in time. I sobbed in relief and buried my face in his chest as he wrapped his arms around me.

That had been close. *Too* close. If I hadn't been watching closely—if I hadn't seen her reach for that knife—that would have been it. Julian would have been dead, and Bridget would have been healed by the gods.

But she'd sacrificed herself when she ran into his knife. So why the sudden change of heart in her final seconds? What had she seen that had made her decide to fight?

I'd never know. But after all of this, there was one thing I knew for sure.

I wasn't going to stand on the sidelines and wait for anyone to protect me ever again. I was going to fight for myself, and I was going to get out of this alive. So were Julian and Cassia. I was going to fight with them until the Nephilim army found us and put an end to this once and for all.

I refused to be a pawn for any longer.

So I pulled myself out of Julian's strong arms, stood up, and faced Octavia.

She sat straight and proud on her throne inside of the Royal Box. The golden wreath gleamed on her head as she looked down at me with pure, unbridled arrogance.

She was enjoying this.

I took a few steps toward her. With each one, my magic buzzed stronger and stronger. It pushed its way out of my palms, two bolts of electricity arcing upward and joining above my head. I fell to my knees, and the magic poured out of me, strands of bright light swirling to create a glowing dome around me.

"You shouldn't have made me your enemy!" I screamed up at Octavia, and the crowd silenced, my voice echoing through the arena. "You underestimated me. But now you see how dangerous I can be. And I won't rest until I make you pay."

39

LILITH

SIX MONTHS AGO

I SAT on the edge of my four-poster bed, admiring the two faerie tokens I held in my palms. They'd taken me years to acquire. I'd run into so many dead ends and false clues. But finally, they were mine.

A familiar knock rapped on the door.

"Come in," I said, and the two people I'd called for stepped inside of my room.

"Fallon," I said to my daughter. With her dark hair, slim figure, and porcelain skin, she was nearly a spitting image of me. "And Lavinia."

The dark witch, Lavinia Foster, could have easily passed as one of my daughters as well. It was thanks to the traces of my family's blood that ran through her—and the rest of the Foster circle's—veins.

"You called?" Fallon asked, her hands resting on her hips in annoyance.

I'd probably interrupted her flirting with one of the many men who passed through the area. Oh well. I was far more important than they could ever be.

"Yes." I opened my fists and revealed the golden tokens, one in each of my palms.

"Faerie tokens," she quickly identified them. "Why…?" She looked to me, leaving the question lingering in the air.

I understood why she was confused. Because as far as she knew, the fae were nothing for us to worry about.

Lavinia, on the other hand, knew differently.

"You found them." Lavinia smiled. "Finally."

Fallon just stared me down, tapping her foot on the ground as she waited for me to explain.

"I'm afraid I've been keeping a secret from you," I told her, and Fallon stilled, like I knew she would. "As you might remember, soon after we came to Earth, we had a gifted vampire under our control. A prophetess."

"Skylar Danvers," Lavinia said proudly. "Her visions were phenomenally accurate. It's a shame we lost her to the Earth Angel."

"It is." I nodded in agreement and turned my attention back to Fallon. "While Skylar was under our control, she was forced to share her visions with

Lavinia, and with Azazel, may he rest in peace." I lowered my eyes in respect for my fallen brother. "There was a pattern to her visions. Whenever she was asked for information about our enemy, she rarely spoke of Avalon. Mostly, she spoke of the fae."

"But we have no qualms with the fae," she said.

"Not yet," I said. "But we cannot ignore the warnings of the prophetess. We *must* take care of the fae. These tokens will transport you and Lavinia to a remote location in the Otherworld, where you'll complete your task of wiping out their entire race."

"Just the two of us?" Fallon looked at me like I'd lost my mind. "How, exactly, are we supposed to do that?"

"As you know, demon blood is poisonous to the fae," Lavinia started.

"Only if they drink it," Fallon interrupted. "And we can't force the *entire Otherworld* to drink my blood. They'll kill us before we get very far."

"That was the challenge," Lavinia said with that knowing smile on her face that I loved so much. "I had to figure out how to get your blood into their systems without putting our lives at risk. It took me many years, and I needed help from others in my circle. But eventually, we created a spell."

"What kind of spell?" At the talk of dark witch magic, Fallon was all ears.

"The perfect spell," I took over from there, eager to be the one to share the news with my daughter. "One that turns our blood into the deadliest, most dangerous of weapons. A highly contagious plague."

I hope you enjoyed The Faerie Pawn! If so, I'd love if you left a review. Reviews help readers find the book, and I read each and every one of them :)

A review for the first book in the series is the most helpful. Here's the link on Amazon where you can leave your review ➜ mybook.to/faeriegames

---

The next book in the series, The Faerie Mates, is out now!

Get your copy now at:
mybook.to/faeriemates

You can also check out the cover and description for The Faerie Pawn below. (You may need to turn the page to view the cover and description.)

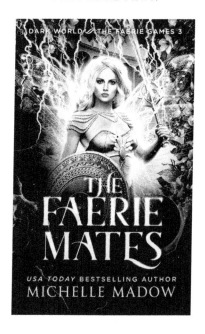

In the Faerie Games, it's kill or be killed. And I'm going to survive, no matter what the cost.

Who will win the next Emperor of the Villa competition? Will I tell Julian that we're soulmates? And most importantly—will Julian, Cassia, and I defeat Octavia and make it out of the Games alive?

I'll do whatever's necessary to survive. Because I'm Selena Pearce—raised by the leaders of Avalon, born of a powerful witch and a faerie prince, and gifted with magic from Jupiter.

And I'm not going to let fear control me any longer.

Get your copy now at:
mybook.to/faeriemates

Also, make sure you never miss a new release by signing up to get emails and/or texts when my books come out!

Sign up for emails: michellemadow.com/subscribe

Sign up for texts: michellemadow.com/texts

And if you want to hang out with me and other readers of my books, make sure to join my Facebook group: www.facebook.com/groups/michellemadow

Thanks for reading my books, and I look forward to chatting with you!

Michelle Madow is a USA Today bestselling author of fast-paced fantasy novels that will leave you turning the pages wanting more! Her books are full of magic, adventure, romance, and twists you'll never see coming.

Michelle grew up in Maryland, and now lives in Florida. She's loved reading for as long as she can remember. She wrote her first book in her junior year of college and hasn't stopped writing since! She also loves traveling, and has been to all seven continents. Someday, she hopes to travel the world for a year on a cruise ship.

Visit author.to/MichelleMadow to view a full list of Michelle's novels on Amazon.

THE FAERIE PAWN

Published by Dreamscape Publishing

Copyright © 2019 Michelle Madow

ISBN: 9781702339834

This book is a work of fiction. Though some actual towns, cities, and locations may be mentioned, they are used in a fictitious manner and the events and occurrences were invented in the mind and imagination of the author. Any similarities of characters or names used within to any person past, present, or future is coincidental.

❋ Created with Vellum

Printed in Great Britain
by Amazon

83203278R00161